T0287882

CANALWATCH

CANALWATCH

Flash Fiction

By

Ken Rivard

mosaic PRESS

Library and Archives Canada Cataloguing in Publication

Title: CanalWatch / Ken Rivard.

Other titles: Canal watch

Names: Rivard, Ken, 1947- author.

Description: Short stories.

Identifiers: Canadiana (print) 20220173125 |
Canadiana (ebook) 20220174261 |

ISBN 9781771616324 (softcover) | ISBN 9781771616331 (PDF) | ISBN 9781771616348 (EPUB) | ISBN 9781771616355 (Kindle)

Classification: LCC PS8585.I8763 C36 2022 | DDC C813/.54—dc23

Published by Mosaic Press, Oakville, Ontario, Canada, 2022.

MOSAIC PRESS, Publishers
www.Mosaic-Press.com

Printed and bound in Canada

ONTARIO ARTS COUNCIL
CONSEIL DES ARTS DE L'ONTARIO
an Ontario government agency
un organisme du gouvernement de l'Ontario

Funded by the Government of Canada
Financé par le gouvernement du Canada

Canada

ONTARIO
CREATES

MOSAIC PRESS
1252 Speers Road, Units 1 & 2, Oakville, Ontario, L6L 5N9
(905) 825-2130 • info@mosaic-press.com • www.mosaic-press.com

OTHER BOOKS BY KEN RIVARD

POETRY

Frankie's Desires (Quarry Press, 1987)
Kiss Me Down To Size (Thistledown Press, 1983)

FICTION

Motherwild (Thistledown Press, 2014)
Missionary Positions (Black Moss Press, 2008)
The Trouble with *Uncle Kevin* (Calgary Communities Against Sexual Abuse, 2007)
Whiskey Eyes (Black Moss Press, 2004)
Bottle Talk (Black Moss Press, 2002)
Skin Tests (Black Moss Press, 2000)
Mom, The School Flooded (Annick Press, 1996, 2007)
If She Could Take All These Men (Beach Holme Publishers, 1995)

This book is for H.P.,
Micheline and canal people everywhere.

Introduction – Author Notes

CANALWATCH IS A COLLECTION OF FLASH FICTION BASED ON observations in or around a mysterious canal that might be found anywhere. Each story of approximately 500 words, is based on the passing image of a particular person, place, event, object or overheard conversation (whether real or imagined) in or around the canal. Readers are invited to sit in the brief story moment of each flash fiction piece. Often the narrative turns back on itself with the first line of the story also becoming the last line, resulting in a kind of story portrait. Not every flash fiction piece progressively builds more tension or moves towards a new understanding because not all of life's moments do that. CANALWATCH is also about the art of wondering, vulnerability, pain, joy, resilience and what it means to be ever so human. Occasionally readers may also be asked to suspend their disbelief. Other times, the point in time being described may appear to be too real to be untrue. Often, a particular idea or moment or image simply asks "what if?" Then the story just takes off and brings readers along for an unusual and imaginative ride. Enjoy the "what if's" and the "not so what if's".

Portions of CANALWATCH have appeared in THE PRAIRIE JOURNAL OF CANADIAN LITERATURE.

Thanks to Brian Brennan for his early editorial comments.

Author photo by Frank O'Donnell.

I would like to acknowledge the following friends for simply being who they are: Lorraine and Wayne Smith... Tania and Frank O'Donnell... Louise Michaud and Rich Willis... Linda and Bill Tymchyshyn. Merci!

Table of Contents

ONE

Hungry For Love 3
An Avalanche Way of Talking 5
Mission 7
Yellow and Other Infinite Piano Variables 9
The Same Truth 11
Her Wall of Breathing 13
That Faint Skittering. 15
Peggy Sue on the Canal 17
Origins 19
Timing 21
Real Deal 23
Legs 25
Women Telling Women 27
Too Good to Be True 29
As Big As Dogs 31
Purse 33
Practicing 35

TWO

Same House of Magic 39
See Ya 41
Perfect 43
Minding Business 45
Murky 47
Up To Here 49
Was It Food? 51
Right Thing 53
I Need More Maturing 55
Decisions 57
The Whiteness 59
Five Orange Pylons and a Red Scooter 61
White-Out 63
Maybe. 65
Discussion. 67
What Do You Hear Right Now? 69
Leftovers 71
What Looks Like 73
Fist Face 75
Wheelchair 77
Limits 79
What the Rain Does 81
Cats and the Suitcase. 83
Canal Lightning 85
Waiting 87
Currents 89
Tugging and Knowing 91

Craving....93
Garage Sale....95
Balloons....97
Ethics....99
Skies and Trains....101
Author....103
The Man and the Eel....105
Stairs....107
Pumpkin Face....109
A Cushion and A Heart....111
Secrets....113

THREE

Changes....117
Being Normal is Over-Rated....119
Are You A Cliché?....121
Corner....123
From The Walls of the Garden Sky....125
Branches....127
Mysteries....129
Fixing....131
Arms....133
Tongues....135
After Thirty-Five Years....137
Canal Hearts....139
Holy Darkness....141
From Disowned to Owned....143
Counting....145
Same Woman....147

I Had No Choice for My Hair Colour....149
Water Prayers....151
Cement Changes....153
The Suitcase....155
Orphan....157
The Lawn Chair....159
My Cravings Are All Yours....161
Bathtubs and Smiles....163
Lilac Woman....165
Even the Homeless....167
A Pee in the Canal....169
My Face is Worth It....171
Critical Acclaim for Ken Rivard's Writing....175

ONE

Hungry for Love

Someone is hungry for love.

Along the canal a man too tall for his bicycle, rides in a slow weave, as if attached to his neck is the longest silk scarf imaginable. Suddenly, he stops not far from me. His bike is painted red and is faded by years of sun while the paint from his fenders clings like loose scabs. He carries a small, aging, green Coleman cooler in one hand while his other hand clings to the handlebar. In his basket are two brown paper bags filled with mysterious shapes. One of the bags is larger than the other and its opening at the top is all scrunched up and pokes at the sky as a corrugated, toy chimney. Lying across the bags is a Barbie Doll which has only one eye, a left eye. Barbie's clothes are worn thin, the colors faded into a pinkish red. Over the missing, right eye is a new, flesh-coloured bandage. The man stops and checks his doll's bandage, as if he knows that Barbie can only handle one half of its perception of the world. After each bump, he probably slowed down and may have said to the toy doll: "Sorry about the rough ride."

The toy could be his only child now or perhaps it is easier to pretend and protect something that can't talk back. I want Barbie to respond to him as I stand there but the toy gives me a blank one-eyed look, as if I should also be the one apologizing for the rough ride.

I stop and the man asks me: "Where do you live?"

"Calgary, Alberta," I say. "Western Canada."

"Is that close to the Rocky Mountains, like Denver?"

"Yes, a city something like Denver, only north."

"Well, I was born right here and I ride around this canal once a day hoping…hoping. You see this doll belonged to my little daughter who drowned last year in this canal. Her body was never found."

"What happened?" I ask gently hoping not to sound intrusive.

"One time I had had too much to drink and went out for a walk with my little girl. She chased a pigeon down the pathway and tripped into the canal. The water level was record high, almost flooding the area at the time and you know how filthy that water is! So I stumbled down those cement stairs and tried to grab her but she sank to the bottom away from me in the surprisingly fast moving current. Nobody could save her. She just floated away from me and I felt it was her time to go. I saved her Barbie Doll though. I've been riding around the canal with the doll in my basket hoping my daughter will somehow float back into my life," he says solemnly as he grips the handlebar. "And I have to watch for the cops because this pathway is for pedestrians only, not bikes, as if that's going to stop me."

It seems as if the sun has been listening to him. Its rays reach down, scoop up his sorrow and spread it along the murky canal, like butter.

"I should get going," says the man. "Thanks for listening."

"You're welcome," I say. "Before you go, what's in that small cooler and those brown bags?"

"A few sandwiches and a bottle of water… in case my daughter comes back to life. She'll be starving. The bags have some dry clothes and shoes for my girl and some extra Barbie Doll clothes."

Pedalling away towards the sun, the man disappears behind a haze. It is so quiet now except for what could be measured sobbing from a passing empty canoe.

Someone is hungry for love.

An Avalanche Way of Talking

THE TEENAGER HAS AN AVALANCHE WAY OF TALKING.

"Listen?" he says. "Bet I can smother you with words."

What could be his identical twin brother sitting beside him on the bench near the canal is tranquil and stares straight ahead and occasionally nods at the words gushing from his brother's lips. The boys look to be about fifteen, and it's the big talker who prefers to share stories about how the two are so much alike. Both boys wear faded blue jeans, white T-shirts and flip-flops.

"Remember the time when we were little and we went to Sear's with Mom and Dad to buy shorts for the summer. I got there first with Dad and he said to pick out four pairs of shorts from a big pile on a table. Digging into the table-top, mound of shorts, I found several pairs and went to try them on. Moments later, you came with Mom and she said the same thing and you went to try them on too. Turned out that we both tried on the same four pairs of shorts and we both ended up choosing the same blue pair. Wasn't that something?"

"Yeah, sure" replies the small talker. "But everyone has heard that twin story."

"Then there was that time when you had your tonsils removed. At the time, I figured that you'd talk even less after you had your tonsils taken out. Crazy, eh? I remember when I was at school and my throat starting hurting so bad, I wanted to rip it out of my neck and I knew right then and there that I'd have to have my tonsils out too. We had so many things happen to us at the same time. I wonder if we'll know when each of us becomes a father? Do you think we live inside each other's brains?"

"I have reasons for being like that though," the big talker says. "Remember Uncle Ray?

"Well, I found out quickly that he was a real sleaze. Whenever he got too close to me, I would tell jokes to keep him away. I'd make up stuff about anything. I'm sure he left me alone because of all my joke-telling. Even today, if I feel that I can't trust someone, I look that person straight in the eye and tell a joke. What about you?"

The quieter of the two boys lowers his head and says: "Uncle Ray tried to touch me once by pretending to tickle me, but I caught on quickly. Whenever he and I were in the same room, I'd stay away from him. Finally, I told Mom and we never saw Uncle Ray again. Mom didn't tell me what she said to him."

Then there is a bigger than big silence between the boys. No strollers. No joggers. Picture-takers become statues near the canal. Winds hold their breaths. Even the few passing motorists cruise by without accelerating. A pigeon stands still at the base of a tall tree, the bird's eyes daring anyone to disturb this moment. The canal waters are so quiet they challenge Uncle Ray to reappear right here under a watchful eye of sun. The two brothers stand and stretch their arms this way and that way. Their sudden laughter sounds tumble over each other. They slap one another on the shoulder. They point up. They point down. Walking away from the canal as casual as can be, the boys tell jokes, laugh and flick their wrists at the freshly washed, cloudless sky and its honest breathing.

"I think I've been inside your brain," the small talker says. Been there and back."

The teenager has an avalanche way of talking.

Mission

WHERE DID HE COME FROM?

The man with a white shirt, black tie and black suit has his grey-brown hair parted perfectly down the middle. He carries a briefcase and steadily moves down the canal, as if he were on a mission of sorts. Into his cellphone, he is clearly heard saying that he doesn't know much about conflict between mothers and sons because he was raised in so many foster homes that each mother was like a bumper in a pinball game that he never won. Then he says to the voice at the other end that he would have been better off with a single, needy mother who taught him to make a list of everything he desired: one mother, one father and maybe a brother or sister. It didn't matter if his only mother wanted, wanted, wanted… as long as she was there. The intimate details of his life are heard everywhere and several small fish in the canal poke their heads out of the water to listen. Even a solitary, flat fish, the length of my lower left arm stops its weaving.

The foster home mothers are a blur to him. What he remembers is that they all waited for that cheque in the mail.

Now the man ambles to a stop and hands out pamphlets for the Jehovah's Witnesses. The church is his mother now and he says to anyone that his mission is brand-new. A young mother pushing her infant in a stroller stops and the man takes that as a sign that she is interested. Pulling several extra pamphlets from his briefcase, the man asks the young woman about her own mother and how she likes being a mother herself. Does a real mother exist?

"Look, I don't know you. Why are you asking?" the young mother asks clutching the handle of her stroller.

"Sorry lady. I didn't mean to scare you or be so personal. I'd like to know about other mothers. Anyhow, here's some reading material for you. It's free."

"Thanks. Oh, yeah, I've seen these before. Usually, you people are standing on street corners," she says handing them back to the man. "No thanks."

"No problem. Do you like being a mom?"

"I live in my motherhood! I'll bet it's the biggest investment I'll ever make in my life."

"Investment…what do you mean?"

Pointing to her son, the woman says, "That boy came out of my body. He is my blood, my DNA! Even you came from a mother somewhere."

"Seriously, I'm not looking for sympathy but I have no idea. I've been in so many mothers' arms, I don't know how it all started for me."

"Aren't you curious about your birth mother?"

"I was just born. I've heard tons of stories about adults searching for and then locating their birth mothers and how disappointed they were. Could be anyone with a vagina and I... ."

"Oh, that's too bad. My own mother is even better than a fake, perfect mother from one of those old TV shows. I'm hoping to do the same with my son."

"Well, my church is now my only mother. I'm determined to make her as real as possible."

"Oh, it's almost lunchtime and my son is crying. I have to get him home. Good luck."

"Thanks. I didn't think I had any mother talk left," the man says.

Where did he come from?

Yellow and Other Infinite Piano Variables

NEAR THE CANAL BRIDGE, A MAN SO TALL HE ALMOST TOUCHES THE leaf of a tree and whose bones protrude like sticks, plops himself on a folding chair and plays his portable keyboard. His hair, the colour of rope, is combed straight back in the sunshine. First, his music floats over the bridge. Then the notes are carried away by the winds and sprinkled over the canal.

"Where did you learn to play like that?" a woman passing by dressed in yellow from head-to-toe asks.

"I played piano before I went to prison," he tells her. "Why do you dress completely in yellow?"

The woman is shocked. Most ex-cons don't tell the world that they just got out of jail but her face is confident as to how she will answer his question.

"You look so sure of yourself," he tells her. "I worked construction but live my whole life for the piano. Yet it was a piano that got me in trouble. I was sitting in a hotel bar with two other construction workers and telling each other how we always took home a souvenir."

"Souvenir… like a glass or mug?"

"Not quite. Near the exit a piano sat quietly and we rolled it outside and loaded it onto our truck."

"Didn't anyone ask questions?" the woman asks.

"Nope. I climbed into the back of the truck and started playing as our truck sped away." "Someone from the hotel must have caught on."

"Yep, and the cops chased us down in no time but I kept playing. They were shocked that I was still able to play anything when they opened the back of the truck."

"So, what happened? But first, have you been in trouble before with the police?" the woman asks her mouth wide open in amazement.

"Because of the piano and my previous problems with the law, I was later sentenced to more time in jail," he tells the woman in yellow. Now, why all this yellow?" he asks.

"Simple. I dress in yellow because it is the brightest of all colours," she says. "It's the colour of happiness, enlightenment, optimism and creativity."

"Please! Yellow can also be the same colour as booze," he says. "And what I leave in the urinal afterwards."

"Surely, there has to be something more," the woman says removing her sunglasses.

"Only piano. Maybe… the only yellow I see is when I touch those worn piano keys."

"If that's the case, then let it be the only colour in your life, like I do."

"But isn't there a dark side to yellow, like a traffic light for caution or being a coward or madness or illness or betrayal?"

"Enough of that. Think instead of sunshine, sunflowers, canaries, the daffodil, egg yolks, bees and, yes even… lemons."

"Want to go for a beer?" he asks her.

"Play me another tune first," she replies her voice as comforting as an easy sky breath. "Play me another."

The Same Truth

THERE SHE IS.

On a bench, a transgendered woman, with an Adam's apple, looking like a tiny piece of fruit, stares into her open purse. Her teak-brown hair falls lightly on the shoulders of her sun yellow blouse and light beige jacket. Her slacks are also the same beige color and they hang perfectly over a dark brown pair of sturdy walking shoes. The woman's nails are bright red and are manicured perfectly; her hands could be on display in a cosmetic department of any retail store. Her make-up is understated except for her shiny, cherry-red lipstick which could also be a STOP sign for someone passing by who might want to share her bench.

The woman sits sideways and is frozen by something inside her purse. Perhaps she cannot find her mirror. Maybe, she is still becoming accustomed to being a woman and the mirror will confirm who she's always wanted to be.

Nobody dares intrude until a pigeon, with equal colours of dirt and white, tip-toes up to her practical walking shoes and then looks up at her purse with a steady eye.

"What do you want, Bird?" the woman asks. "Can't you see that I'm looking for something?" The pigeon bobs its head up and down and then lowers its beak to several bread crumbs lying a short distance from the woman's shoes.

"Go ahead. Eat up those crumbs," she says. "But don't peck at my shoes. They're expensive!" The bird looks at one of her shoes and then the other while swallowing crumbs.

"What's on your mind, Bird? And stop studying my neck like that, will ya!"

The pigeon moves towards her right shoe and pecks away at several bread crumbs directly behind the heel of the same shoe.

"Where did I put that mirror anyway?" the woman asks herself.

Then the bird struts to the toe of her left shoe and searches for more crumbs.

"Do you have any idea what I've been through? Do you? Yeah, ever since I can remember I never felt like a guy. It's the usual story- I didn't know what I felt like but it wasn't a male. Then, when I was twenty, I could strongly feel a woman inside me. A few years after that, I had the surgery. Can you see my truth? Can you? Let me share that with you. That's what draws people to be friends, you know. Friends see the same truth. Will you be my friend for now?"

As if the bird understood, it stands still right between the woman's two sensible shoes and coos gently at her.

"Yes, you are my friend and look… here's my mirror!" the woman says.

With the small mirror in her hand, she checks her hair, her eyes, her forehead, her nose, her mouth and her chin. Then her mirrored hand freezes at her throat.

"This Adam's apple could only belong to a man. I need more follow-up. The doctor told me that he would have to do some finishing touch-ups."

"Coo, Coo, Coo," the pigeon says.

"Yes, I'm hoping the rest of my manhood will be gone forever."

Slipping her mirror back into her purse, the woman rubs her Adam's apple with her left hand and then clamps her purse shut.

The lump in her throat sags slightly. The crumbs are gone. And so is the bird.

Her Wall of Breathing

"JUST FOLLOW THE GLARE."

Overlapping the bench, like a flat, white tongue, the woman's skateboard hangs in the afternoon air with its fin gleaming in the sunlight. The woman, who might be in her mid-forties, has wild reddish hair and wears a fitted, black outfit meant to protect her skin from weather. Some of her hair is tied up in a ponytail fist half-way up the back of her head. Her eyes out-brown the soil near the bench and they shine with confidence. With one arm around her skateboard, the woman grins at each and every passerby, as if she were offering her joy to anyone and everyone.

They all know she's the one who lives on her skateboard. Chances are that many in the crowd have seen or heard about her on the canal pathway. Even senior citizens are glued to their binoculars after they see her skate by.

When she lowers herself, the woman is soon joined by dogs and cats moving towards her. The stillness of the animals becomes the woman's stillness. The wind laps gently over her board. The dogs and cats pause together with her, as if they are all preparing to go through a carwash of sorts. Then all of the animals, with their heads below the wind, inhale and exhale in unison. Joining the animal breathing, the woman is transformed into such a calm state that a halo takes shape above her skateboard.

Although she now sits on a bench with her board, the winds appear to have followed the woman to her bench and reach over the canal. A crowd gathers nearby to wonder what's next.

“I don’t belong on this bench,” she tells the crowd. “I was simply walking home to my apartment with my skateboard and stopped for a moment. Why are you all gathered around me?”

A man and woman both seniors and wearing large-brimmed Panama hats look first at each other and then the skateboarder.

“You shouldn’t be here. You belong on the pavement,” the woman senior says. “I can tell.”

“That’s true,” the man senior adds. “Look at all these people standing here. They know where you really live. Forget your apartment.”

“Right, get on your skateboard,” a young businesswoman points to the nearby sidewalk. “It’s home.”

Other people offer more encouragement and the skateboarder is amazed at how their messages are the same. “How can you tell?” she asks aloud.

A woman jogger in her mid-twenties, dressed in a mid-blue sweatsuit and navy-blue jogging shoes, points to several people in the crowd.

“It’s obvious to us that you’re a fish out of water when just sitting on that bench, like that Hollywood movie. You’re smiling lots but your body looks tight and out of place. And the way you’re holding that skateboard makes me think that it’s another layer of skin for you!”

“Yeah, I’m surprised that you don’t have wings to go along with your lungs,” a man laughs with a belly overlapping his belt and eating a chocolate ice cream cone announces between licks. “Come on, let’s get you moving. We’ll follow.”

The woman skateboarder stands and lifts her long, narrow board to the top of her head with a hand gripping each side to keep the board balanced. She is ready to drop her board and jump on.

“You’re right. Come with me,” she says.

That Faint Skittering

ALONG THE NORTH SIDE OF THE CANAL ARE VARIOUS LITTLE GARDENS four deep, each one about ten feet long and ten feet wide, each a tiny sanctuary. Each plot is fenced in. Some have pots hanging from rope or wire. Many contain either a chair or a small bench. A couple have wooden shelves along a fenced wall containing some garden supplies. Access to a community hose is used by gardeners to grow mostly flowers and other plants.

In one garden an Asian woman, who could be forty or seventy years of age, tends to her growing crop. Angrily, she clears the soil of weeds and slowly fondles each and every surviving plant, like a sacred object and then gently sprinkles water on each one.

Her garden has been mostly destroyed by nighttime rats. An elderly Asian man shuffling by with his cane asks her in very simple English what she has done to protect her garden.

"Rats, what they do at night?" he asks with certainty, as if the woman couldn't possibly understand him right away.

The woman points to sheets of hard red plastic that she has placed around the bottom half of her fence to keep the rodents out and then throws up her hands to the setting sun, as if the plastic has not been remotely successful. After, she bends over and picks up two containers of poison placed in the corners of her garden and then puts the containers back. The woman bends over again and picks up two dead rats by their tails, looks around to make sure no one is watching and then flings the rodents over her garden fence onto the canal pathway-...an action that the police might not appreciate but probably understand. Over in the other two corners of her garden, she has more poison but only finds one carcass to fling into the sky. Much of her lush, green produce has been eaten. Several plants have been chewed unevenly, some almost down to the soil. The woman wrings her hands, turns her back to the canal and then goes to sit on her tiny wooden bench. She mutters to herself and pulls out a small handgun from her purse. Pointing the handgun in her right hand at the garden, the woman then lifts her short legs onto the bench. Looks like she plans to spend the night here and make sure no more bites are taken in her garden. And if they try, she will use her handgun together with a small flashlight from her purse in her left hand. Her back is braced straight up against the inside arm of her bench. The woman has even brought her supper in a brown bag and decides to eat it all just as the sun sets the western sky ablaze. She even saves a few leftovers to spread on the ground, maybe to entice more beady-eyed visitors to her garden.

The quick, pure darkness settles over the canal and the winds have curled into their quiet language under the moon and stars. With her handgun and flashlight ready, the woman watches and waits. The elderly man with the cane is long gone; he lives across the street on the south side of the canal and he may be waiting for the sound of gunshots. For a few minutes, the pathway is empty and quiet. Floating by the woman and her garden with a slow, silent pace, the canal is ready for that faint skittering, for a gun being cocked.

Peggy Sue on the Canal (for L.S.)

WHY DOES EVERYONE KNOW PEGGY SUE'S FACE?

There she is sitting quietly on a canal bench wearing a blue and white checkered shirt and absorbed in a murder-mystery book. Most people who stop by do so because they say Peggy Sue reminds them of someone they know. She just has one of those looks.

One woman, who has a southern accent as thick as molasses, plunks herself down beside Peggy Sue and immediately wraps an arm around her, as if Peggy Sue were as familiar as DNA.

"Y'all my sweetie because I like murder-mystery books too," she tells Peggy Sue.

Right away, Peggy Sue's face shows an elevator of red colour moving upward from her chin to her forehead.

"I haven't seen you in ages, darlin'. Where have you been?" the woman continues.

But Peggy Sue is too much of a mix of shyness and hidden laughter to tell the woman that she's never met her before in her life so she slides away to the far end of the bench and the safety of her book. "Guess ya need to climb back into your story so I better get going. See you later darlin'" the woman with the thick accent says before getting up and resuming her walk.

Moments later, a middle-aged man wearing a straw hat, jean shorts and a gold-coloured T-shirt, stops directly in front of Peggy Sue and takes hold of her right hand.

"So glad to see you again, you amazing woman, you!" he says with a smile as wide as her book. Peggy Sue closes her book with her free hand and looks up at the stranger.

"Who… are you?' she asks her face already tomato-red.

"Don't you remember me?" he says. "I used to go to all your high school basketball games. I cheered for you louder than anyone in the gym. You were that good! Sometimes we talked when I waited for you after you came out of the dressing-room. You… looked spectacular back then too."

"Sorry, I don't remember you," Peggy Sue replies, her ears a blotchy red.

"Ernest. My name is Ernest," he says. "I went to Three Rivers High School, like you."

This time Peggy Sue lets go of the man's hand and holds her closed book to her chest with both hands. The man says: "Don't mean to embarrass you and this may not be the right thing to say but… you still look sensational, Peggy Sue. See you."

Several minutes later, after Peggy Sue's face has lost its September apple colour, she lowers her eyes to her murder-mystery story again.

Twice in a row, dogs stop directly in front of Peggy Sue and place both front paws on her bench, almost begging her to take them in her arms. Each time she rolls her eyes back into her head, as if saying to the world: "Oh, no, not another animal wanting to be on my lap." But then she looks at each of the dog owners with eyes that say: "I just love all dogs," as if contradiction is her middle name.

When she is finally alone, Peggy Sue can be heard talking to nobody in particular. "I love murder-mystery novels when at the end, the bad guy gets stabbed with a screwdriver!"

Peggy Sue might seem like someone who is subdued about life and she rarely pushes people away. Yes, everyone might know Peggy Sue and that she lives between the colours of black and white but her bond paper-white, face isn't sure about all the knowing.

Why does everyone know Peggy Sue's face?

Origins

HER INTENTIONS ARE CLEAR.

Leaning against a tree overlooking the canal, a blonde-haired, young mother cradles her infant in the crux of her right arm and tells inquisitive passersby that HE is a good boy. The baby is fast asleep but has the beginnings of two tears dripping down his cheeks from closed eyes. The woman's intense blue eyes are filled with concern. Almost immediately, she makes her son's pain her pain. Her left hand is almost at her mouth as she too is about to shed her own discomfort out of frustration. Hoping to take away all of her baby's hurt, she is desperate and will do anything and thinks of waking him so she can stop his jerking eyelids. But maybe those tears have nothing to do with agony. The top of the blue baby blanket will not absorb the warm wetness and each globule lies like a tiny unanswered question. The mother sees her reflection in each tear and wonders whether she passed on any of her ancient torment to her son. Did his dreaming start in her womb or is she making too big a deal out of all this?

"Please wake up, Son, so I can understand your silent crying," the mother carefully whispers, as if she's not sure if she wants her boy to be awake or not. She lets him sleep more under the shade of the tree and hopes that the tears will stop shortly. After all, it could be a bad dream or perhaps some explosive joy that will pass within seconds. The mother gently dabs his cheeks with a tissue and then does the same with her own face. Then she holds her baby closer to her chest, maybe hoping the warmth of her left breast might find a way to wake him to his own hunger.

"Just because he can't tell me about his dream doesn't mean that he's not dreaming," she may be saying to herself.

Perhaps the infant may not yet have a strong sense of self, or other people, or of objects around him so his dreams may be silent. Or he may only dream of sucking, crying and pooping. Maybe his mother shows up in the dream or maybe the cat. Finally, she simply lets her child dream himself out.

The infant opens his eyes and she offers him her breast while covering herself with the blanket. Eventually, the salty fluid has stopped completely and his eyes are half-open in mother's milk contentment. His cheeks move in and out and his skin is the colour of freshly-picked peaches. Whatever the baby experienced earlier has vanished. Still, the mother is curious. She would do anything to prevent anymore hurt from happening to her child and maybe she promises herself that her son will never go hungry or require a change of diapers when she's not there. Perhaps the problem may have been cramps, a fever, rash, or colic issues. Some say that babies have no real fears until the ages of two or three so there's a good chance the baby boy did not have a scary dream. But if he wasn't frightened, what was it? Could it be outside traffic or unsettling mother noises that disturbed him? No, this mother looks like she practices some form of meditation because her own breathing sounds so measured, so reassuring. And the mid-afternoon traffic on the boulevard next to the canal moves quietly except for the occasional moped accelerating past a slow-moving vehicle.

The mother moves away from the tree, her son now satiated and his eyelids becoming heavy again. She walks down towards the canal itself and smiles broadly at two teenage girls in a canoe paddling their way eastward with silent confidence.

"Humm," she says aloud. "I'm so glad I did nothing."

Her intentions are clear.

Timing

SHE'S READY.

On a small hill overlooking the canal, a pregnant woman sitting with her legs outstretched, pulls up her black T-shirt and thrusts her swollen belly at the sun. Strapped to her left wrist is a ticking stop-watch, like an involuntary muscle belonging to no one. The woman's face stares straight at the sun as her long, cocoa-coloured hair hangs over her right shoulder as a thick ponytail. She wears pants that could be pyjama bottoms and are covered with many rainbow-coloured lizards and frogs. Her long thumbs press gently on her belly and the tall grass around her is in need of trimming as it waves to anyone who stops to look. Perhaps the woman is cautious about the sunlight on her skin or she is timing the performance of the sudden ballet of head and legs inside her stomach. On her feet are half-hidden, black canvas shoes.

Near the middle of her balloon-white belly there is movement beneath the skin. The tiny shape of what might be a foot is seen pushing against the woman's whiteness. The infant is ready to take a first step into the world and the expectant mother lowers her head slightly to place a light index fingertip on the moving bulge. She grazes the foot with a loving finger as the foot moves up and down. The foot stops and then continues its slight bulging, as if it were telling its mother that it already had a plan for its life. The woman removes her fingertip and traces a lifeline between sunbeams that may or may not happen for her child. Perhaps she wonders if she and her child will see eye-to-eye about conceivable directions.

"Why am I even thinking about all this when all I want is for the kid to be born healthy," she says aloud as she blinks away the sun's insistent glare.

Then there is a larger bulging from her stomach which must be the baby's head. The woman would love to lower her own head so it would be next to the baby's but that is physically impossible so she uses the same finger to trace the circumference of her child's head.

"Maybe the baby will have its father's big head… seven and three-quarter inches all around," she laughs. "Hopefully not as big as one of those plastic ice cream buckets."

Soon she gently places two then three fingers on the baby's head and strokes it ever so slightly. "Can you read my thoughts little one?" she asks her voice like a wafer of warmth. "I'm waiting for you. It's been a long pregnancy but please… don't rush!"

The shape of the baby's head disappears and the woman turns her belly to the right to allow the sun to warm that side of her. Then she carefully outlines shapes of lizards and frogs on that side of her stomach maybe because she has a fascination with certain cold-blooded creatures. The woman checks to see if there is any resemblance to the reptile shapes on her pants. Perhaps she plans to decorate her baby's room with decals of reptiles because she figures that their cold blood will keep her baby's unpredictable body temperature at a safe level. Just the image or thought of a reptile reassures her.

Later, the expectant mother turns her belly to the left and there is no movement below the skin. She rests both hands on her quiet belly and gently sings a lullaby.

Winds passing over the canal cradle her song and then carry it across to the other side, like a mother song being released to the world. At last, she gets to her feet and checks her wristwatch, as if time itself had stopped so the woman could create her own season before birth. Then she tugs at her black T-shirt because the woman loves her belly's modesty, a meekness without pretension.

She's ready.

Real Deal

Tap! Tap! Tap!

A tall, black-eyed woman in her early twenties with her green-coloured hair spiked up to the sky, looks as if she might be composing a text message to her boyfriend on her designer smartphone. Her hair swings between the lines of her message like a pendulum. Frantic are the woman's fingers. With eyes blazing, her lips mouth the words of her text message. Her feet move down the steps to the water. There the woman paces back and forth on the bottom step of a stairway and soon she steps straight into the canal. Fortunately, the water is shallow by the wall today and she is up to her knees, captured by her message and the water. She screams, stops, climbs back onto the bottom step and turns right back up the stairs. Then she parks herself on a bench where she removes her sandals. Luckily, the woman is wearing shorts but her sandals are covered in sludge so she pulls them off her feet, shakes them and flings them onto the grass near the bench.

"Are you okay?" an older woman passing by asks. "I saw what happened." The second woman is dressed in a navy business suit, sturdy black pumps and carries a dark brown leather briefcase; she lives to work.

"It's my boyfriend," the barefoot woman says. "Most days I can't stand being away from him. My texting to him is non-stop!"

"Why?" the second woman asks. "Hope I'm not being nosey?"

"Not really. All I know is that we can't keep our hands off each other. Our passion is like a drug. There is urgency, intensity and I make high-risk choices with him. I forget about what's important to me. I'm not sure if our relationship is solid… you know…the real deal."

The second woman stands back and there is a red glow on her cheeks. This is far too much information.

The woman with the bare feet may be on fire but the other woman in the business suit is frozen there on the path.

"Does it feel like you are caring about your best friend?" the businesswoman asks while pushing her eyeglasses further up her nose.

"Not sure. I do know that my brain becomes numb but that feeling is only temporary."

"Do you think about his feelings before you act?"

"Most times I only care about what's going to happen right now between us."

"Do you have a passionate concern for his well-being?" the businesswoman asks.

"Only when I don't get enough sex from him," answers the text messenger with a calculated grin.

"Well, you've just answered your own question. Anyhow, I have to go. I have to meet someone." The woman with the designer smartphone watches it light up with another text message. Her phone's hot but she holds back and lets her phone absorb the heat.

"What happens between me and him happens fast," she says aloud to the back of the other woman walking away into the uneven sunlight.

Then the texting woman reaches for her sandals, inspects each one and flings them into the canal. As she herself prepares to leave, the woman scoops up her smartphone and tosses it over the canal. But a strong wind returns the phone to her, like a boomerang, and smacks her across the forehead.

"What the hell!" she screams plopping herself back down on the bench and rubbing her head. Then the smartphone rings again... and again...and again.

Tap! Tap! Tap!

Legs (for M.)

Is she addicted to something?

The woman on the bench by the canal may be hooked on this particular book because not one of the people walking or running by distracts her from the page. Maybe she is a curious and also an articulate, ludic reader, someone who reads several books a week. The woman appears to be playful about her reading too because she is totally absorbed but there is a quiet, whimsical bliss flooding its colours on her face. Her right leg is crossed over her left leg and she casually wiggles the toes on her right foot, as if the toes are enjoying her story too. Perhaps the woman is being transported to a place where joy needs no admission ticket.

She wears black shorts, mid-brown coloured sandals and a white-T-shirt. She is about five feet, six inches tall, has blonde streaked, dark brown hair and large curious eyes that may have been weaned on fascination. Her accent, olive skin colour and dark features might also indicate that she has some Latina in her blood.

I stop not far from her and say: "Sorry to interrupt but it looks like a great read."

"Yes, it certainly is," she replies looking straight up at me and not the least bit annoyed. "The story is about a widow who invites a long-time widower neighbour to come and spend the night in her bed… just to talk, of course. And the story develops its own leg life from there. Maybe you've seen the film?"

"No, I haven't. My legs are almost there myself," I say. "But I really don't know what my own age is supposed to look or feel like. I asked my family doctor not long ago and he just laughed at my question and told me that my legs belong to a much younger person - whatever that means."

"People say my legs are fine," she says. "For a moment there, I thought you were staring at my legs and I didn't like it. After talking with you I see that you're not a sleazy man."

High in the sky directly above the canal, a small plane has a banner tied to its tail. The banner reads: "STAYRITE DRY-CLEANING - DROP YOUR PANTS HERE!"

"Someone up there has a sense of humour," I say to the woman.

"Right," she says. "Except for gender and race issues, all this political correctness has its place but may be squeezing the laughter out us," she says.

"Really?" I ask.

"Yes. I want to get back to my book."

"Sure. Enjoy."

I look up at the small plane which has circled in the west and is ready to cut back over the canal. The white dry-cleaning banner, covered with its message in bright red letters, is flat against the sky. Then I look down at my own legs. My legs are happy legs and they want to keep moving.

As I turn to leave, the ludic reader woman asks me my name and I ask for hers.

Suddenly my legs want to go nowhere and the woman stands up.

"Want to go for a walk?" she asks. "Just a short one as I'm busy today."

"Really?" I ask. "I don't want to take you away from your story."

"No problem. My story has nowhere to go. For now."

Is she addicted to something?

Women Telling Women (for Dave Foraie)

In a café on the boulevard, just south of the canal, a group of women share lunch and the conversation around their table could light up the sky. The youngest woman, perched on a brown leather stool cushion, is somewhat removed from the group, and her dress is so short, her thighs never end. With her right foot turned partially upward, an ankle bracelet hangs like a coded message to the sun. This woman has her back to a yellow wall that holds the shadow of a menu opened on a white wooden stand. Above the group of women, tree branches hollow out the wall, branches digging for something.

Behind the spindle-covered, cafe window, a lone waiter stands at a counter with a glowing light bulb over his head that may be trying to highlight his thoughts. Perhaps, the waiter awaits a final order from the women outside and he pauses while listening intently to their talking.

The woman in a white blouse at the table outside has just forked some food into her mouth and her eyes are as wide as her water glass. Above this woman's head, the shape of a large leaf stands tall; a shadow on guard duty. What is she hearing from the woman dressed in dark brown directly in front of her?

"Caught my lover in bed with a younger woman a few nights ago," the woman in dark brown tells the group matter-of-factly. Instead of trying to make excuses, he invited me into bed with him and the younger woman. Turned out that the younger woman preferred me to my lover so together we ignored him. As he calmly got dressed, he watched the two of us seeking pleasure that only we knew. So, I'd like you all to meet Lisette, my new lover" she says pointing to the young woman with the never-ending thighs.

"What happened to your old lover?" another woman dressed in pale green asks.

"Gone forever I hope," says the woman in the dark brown outfit. "I never liked sharing myself with more than one person at a time."

"Do you feel sad?" someone else inquires.

"Not in the least! Besides, he's Swiss and not a good lover. Maybe he should stick to being an organizer. Not a drop of French blood in him."

The entire table explodes with laughter and two of the women almost choke on their food. "Let's hope there are no Swiss people listening," one of the women says wiping the laughter tears from her eyes.

"Lisette must be French?"

"Oui," Lisette answers. "From Montreal; you know The Montreal Canadiens, The Habs."

Then each woman studies one another for a brief moment in silence. Inquisitive winds curl their way across the table, like tiny hands as the women finish their food and order another glass of wine.

Lisette cannot take her eyes off the woman in dark brown.

"Anything else?" the waiter asks.

"No, just a final glass of wine, please" the woman in pale green answers. "And then our bill."

"Sure. Hope you all have a great day!"

"We will," Lisette and the woman in dark brown reply at almost the same time.

Right above Lisette's head, two silhouettes on the wall become something extraordinary, something that will take more time to define.

Too Good to Be True

THE SUN IS UP TO SOMETHING.

In the early morning there is an unusual smokiness draped over the canal when looking eastward. Is that rising sun causing this blur or is it something else? Whatever happens, the winds are returning later this morning and they will remove any doubts about mist and sunlight.

After pushing her way through the haze, an Asian woman emerges with her entire body, except her face, covered in, what looks like, transparent black cotton. I realize from her movements that her only intention is to march away from the blaring sun splashing its yellow on her back. Then she stops, looks down the stairs leading to the water and watches two teenage boys standing opposite one another listening to The Eagles *Hotel California* pounding from a boom-box.

I too stop and listen to the music.

"Why do you walk with your back to the sun?" I ask the woman.

"Protection," she answers quickly. "I don't trust the harshness."

"Why?"

"Sometimes it's too strong and other times it's too sudden or it hides."

"What do you mean?"

"One minute it hides behind clouds easing over the island. Then the clouds burn off over the canal and the sun reappears overpowering the sky. Afterwards, that same sun may remain as is or it might slide under another cloud. Yes, most days the sun burns off any semblance of cloud. Still, you can't predict what it's going to do. And the winds can make a difference too."

"But aren't there winds everywhere?"

"Not like the winds here," she replies. "So, I need to protect myself and my skin by dressing in black."

Hotel California has ended and both boys look up at us.

"You two like music?" the taller of the two boys asks as he runs his hand through his orange tipped hair.

"I do anyway," I say. "That song was really popular in the nineteen seventies and it seems that people still like to hear it."

"Maybe that song's too good to be true, like the sun," the woman says.

"Now why would you say that?" I ask.

But the woman in black doesn't answer. She walks away from me again with her back to the sun. The canal glows from the early daylight and the gauze lifts.

Down on the steps the two boys play the song again. I listen and turn my face to the sunlight. I walk back up the steps and continue moving towards the brightness.

"Enjoy the song, boys," I say.

The woman in black has gone. I can see her in the distance, like a tall, dark, but shadowy illustration on the cover of a book, turning right to cross over to the north side of the canal. Soon she will have to, at least partially, face the natural light and then perhaps the story in that song will make some sense to her. Then I smile at all the good and bad hotel songs and stories I know. I'm in a few of them myself. Some I recall. Some I try to forget. Some want to forget me.

The sun is up to something.

As Big as Dogs

For sure she knows the night.

A woman, who may have been born in unshakeable skin, walks her dog along the canal at night and she suddenly freezes when she notices a hoard of rats moving towards her and her pet. Her mid-sized pet snarls and the rats form a half-circle around the woman and her dog. The woman looks frantic and tugs at her animal's leash so they can escape. She cuts across the grass surrounding the canal pathway and waits for a break in the traffic heading west on the boulevard. The dog turns and snarls at the tiny-legged night. Then the woman bolts across the boulevard with her dog beside her. A man on a pale blue Harley Davidson motorcycle almost hits the dog and a tourist in a red jeep swerves just in time. This was supposed to be a break in traffic but the motorcycle and jeep came out of a nowhere side street. In the darkness, she shouts: "No more walking my dog here at night. Those rats are almost as big as half-grown dogs!"

The woman sits on the second step leading up to an apartment building on the opposite side of the boulevard with her dog nestled close to her. Her breathing is heavier than the night which is devoid of any movement. Across the boulevard, the rats have vanished, perhaps afraid of being run over by motor vehicles. Or maybe they've gone searching for another dog walker.

The canal pathway appears to be calm. The night breathes on its own. On her lap, the dog rests its head. Both the woman and her dog slowly exhale at each other.

The dog lifts its head and hears the woman going back to her childhood. "When I was a girl, I remember listening to the rats running under our bedroom floor on winter nights when they'd come out looking for food. I tried holding a pillow over my head or sticking my fingers in my ears to block out the rat noises. It sounded like there were tons of them running under our wooden floor. My little sister was fast asleep in the folding bed across from my bed. Maybe she was too young to be disturbed by these nightly sounds. A few nights later the rats were louder than usual so I got out of bed and ran into the kitchen where my father was reading a biography of Winston Churchill at the kitchen table.

We have to move out of this apartment because the rats will soon be in our bedroom," I told him.

"Well, that did it! Within a few days, on his Thursday night bowling league night, my father found someone who was willing to rent a place to us for May 1st, we were packed up and moving to another rental. Since then, the last time I saw a rat was when I was fifteen and helping my cousin move some stuff from a barn when a rat ran up my pant leg. Beautiful, eh?"

The woman is up on her feet and saying to her dog: "Enough of the past. Let's get going. We're not done our walk yet."

They walk eastward along the boulevard thinking that all is well until they come across the body of a dead rat on the sidewalk. The dog stops and growls again. The woman too comes to a halt. Then she takes aim at the dead rodent with her right foot and boots the rat straight up in the air. As the carcass floats over the passing traffic, the night slowly inhales its darkness. Even the night time traffic suddenly becomes snail-like so drivers can witness the rodent's slow arcing.

For sure she knows the night.

Purse

WHAT WILL HER LIPS SAY?

A woman with cheeks sprinkled with freckles, sits stone-like on the bench facing the canal with another older woman who might be her mother. The daughter, with her open purse beside her, moves her lips in silence, as if rehearsing what she might say to her mother.

A third woman barely out of her teens and looking exhausted after a long jogging session, needs to stop and rest so she squeezes in beside mother and daughter… three people now stuffed onto one bench. The woman with freckles has her open purse on the bench and the handbag is nudged by the third woman because of limited space.

"Stay away from my purse!" the woman says.

The third woman apologizes and suggests that the first woman move her handbag onto her lap which is what happens next.

"I don't appreciate anyone touching my purse."

"I understand," says the jogger. "I'll be on my way."

The jogger stands and wipes her forehead with her right arm.

"Have a good day," the jogger says about to resume her running.

But the purse owner's face is now so contorted, she is on her feet waving her open handbag at the sky. "I can't take this," she yells at her mother. "My purse has been touched by someone else."

"Easy does it. Even as a child, you never liked people touching anything that belonged to you," the mother says calmly patting her daughter on the shoulder.

"But that jogger was also a stranger!"

"Tell me, what did her touching do?" the mother asks.

"My handbag has been contaminated. Germs! I need to start over."

The purse owner is now on her feet and moving to the canal's edge. Then she empties her entire handbag into the canal.

"Nothing in this bag belongs to me anymore."

Then the woman takes a final look into her empty purse and also flings it into the water.

"There. Done," she says after turning to face her mother.

"You just threw away your wallet, all of your I.D's., your house keys, car keys… all of your belongings!"

"I know. I know."

"What's next?"

"I would like to become someone else."

"And who would that be?" the mother inquires.

Frantically pacing back and forth on the canal pathway, the daughter fills her lungs with the freshness of incoming winds while hugging what could be an imaginary, ultimate purse.

On the boulevard, the continuous honking of a solitary vehicle pierces through the sunlight, like an ice pick. A middle-aged moped driver parks his bike close to a tree and looks at the daughter perhaps wondering what's next. In the ultra-blue sky, a cloud is a milky question mark. Even the surface of the canal is a huge maze of queries.

"Sorry I asked," the mother finally blurts out. "I just realized something about you."

What will her lips say?

Practicing

THIS IS THE LANGUAGE OF THESE FACES.

A middle-aged woman in an apple-red dress covered with blue and white Hibiscus flowers stops at a canal bench occupied by a young gay couple who could be very recent newlyweds. The two men point and laugh at cellphone photographs and their fingers trace love letters on each other's faces.

"Good day, gentlemen!" the woman says to the couple. "I grew up with lots of family warmth and I want to pass it on to you both. Would you like some?"

The incredibly fit couple may be weight lifters and the gym could be their church. They might be from an Eastern European country and don't quite understand the woman's words. But they smile back while nodding at her, as if on cue. The three of them keep bowing at each other until exhaustion sets in and they all finally dissolve into laughter.

"My family warmth welcomes you to the canal. Please feel the offering of my love to you. We are all family here around the canal."

The taller of the two men who may know some very basic English finally says, "Thank... you."

"You... have... family?" the woman asks.

The two men point at each other and graze one another's face with more fingertips.

"You...have...each...other," she says.

"Thank... you," the taller man repeats.

Then the woman carefully sits next to the two men and, using sign language, asks if they would share their cellphone photos with her.

The men's faces say they are delighted because their cheeks reach up to their eyes. Cellphone pictures show the two men exchanging rings at a city hall which certainly doesn't look like City Hall here. Then there are photos of the reception afterwards and of the two men at their airport preparing to leave for a honeymoon. After that, more photos of their hotel room, having dinner together and individual pictures of the men lying by a swimming pool. The most common feature of all their photos is that there are no rehearsed or pasted smiles anywhere.

"Thank you for your joy," the woman says.

"Thank you," the taller man repeats.

"Thank you for your thank yous," the woman adds laughing at her own words.

The men look momentarily confused but pocket their cellphones and stand together in front of the woman. Then they turn and walk westward side-by-side with arms clasped around each other's waists. Occasionally, one man smiles at the other and their eyes light up the canal with determination. Both men head off into the bright afternoon, now hip to hip, shoulder to shoulder.

Back at the bench, the woman folds her hands in a non-stop celebration. An elderly couple out for a canal stroll can't help but slow down, and they fall completely under her warm, family spell. Two teenage boys on skateboards know they shouldn't be on the path meant for pedestrians only, stop, pick up their skateboards and give a "thumbs-up" to the woman. Finally, from the opposite direction, the two gay men return and immediately surrender to the woman, as if gratitude can only be an action word.

This is the language of these faces.

TWO

Same House of Magic

THERE IS A TRICK TO ALL OF THIS. THERE IS.

Perched on a slight hill of grass above the canal, I hear a young woman speaking earnestly to her probable mother on a bench not far from where I am.

In her mid-twenties, the woman is so tall and slender that if she turned sideways, the wind would blow her off her feet. Her straw-like hair is tied back in a ponytail and held together with a cherry-red band. She is dressed fashionably in a beige track suit and white running shoes that look like they came right out of the box. As each sentence spills out of her mouth, her arms and hands chop through the afternoon air and the mother follows her daughter's movements...an intimate sign language between mother and daughter.

The mother wears a white sun hat covering her charcoal grey hair and oversized sunglasses. Her long-sleeved blouse is filled with brown or red triangles and circles. Her slacks are chocolate brown in colour and they hang perfectly above mid-brown, very sensible, walking shoes. With hands folded almost in prayer on her lap, even her ring-filled fingers seem to be paying attention to her daughter.

"When Dad first started as a magician, he was delightful. Later on, when he became very silent at home, a grey cloud pushed its way into the room and I knew what was coming next. Whenever that cloud appeared, I talked fast to prevent the inevitable. Or, I'd get someone else in the room to talk in order to keep the explosion inside dad's magician head. Don't you remember his tricks, Mom?"

The mother's head drops to her chest, like a bag of plums. She unfolds her hands and studies the rings on her fingers carefully. Lifting her head, the mother uncrosses her legs and says: "You certainly were the big watcher and talker in our house back then. That's for sure."

"Do you remember why, Mom?"

"I recall your father coming home from doing his magician act and his nerves would be shot. He rarely talked and just needed some time alone after working on stage. Never did find out what happened to him during his performances. Remember how he'd go to the basement to be on his own for a while telling us that he had to perfect a new trick before bed?"

"Yes, I remember that part, but tell me, Mom… where were you when all this was happening?"

"What do you mean? I saw what was going on. Sure, your father had a temper that would come out of nowhere but he never once hit me. Never! He was an artist. I do know that there was something going on between you and him. Maybe, you just didn't get along. Let it go! Your father's dead."

"No," the daughter says. "You weren't always there when I asked him about the secrets behind his tricks. And there's something else, Mom. After, I went to see a therapist and I sat in a huge stuffed black leather chair while hugging a teddy bear, I told her about Dad's dark magic. But you don't want to discuss it because the truth is the problem!"

"Enough! No more!" the mother shouts sitting bolt upright on the bench and abruptly twisting her rings back and forth on her fingers. "He's gone! So are his tricks. Maybe you should go on Dr. Phil."

A pigeon, with a dark gray patch on its chest, struts over to their bench and eyes first the young woman and then her mother, as if the bird were wisdom on claws. Soon the pigeon jerks its head back and forth, like a stutter, until the young woman gets up and walks away, her shoulders slumped…two lost waves on the canal.

There is a trick to all of this. There is.

See Ya

"SEE YA," I SAY.

In the early morning light, a puddle of vomit, the size of a large frying pan, covers the path around the canal. I wonder if it is the result of some late-night partying when I come across a homeless man sleeping on a bench with today's open newspaper covering his face. Stopping my walk, I get a sour whiff of the vomit. I hear his voice under the newspaper mumbling that it's safer for him, as a homeless man, to sleep during the day.

"Why is that?" I ask.

"Sometimes people get robbed, beaten and raped at night even if they think they are safer sleeping on a bench. The only safe part of sleeping at night on a bench is that the rats can't bite you. If a guy sleeps on the grass, say under a tree, the rats will eat the cartilage on the end of his nose or the bottom flaps of the ears or that fleshy part between the thumb and first finger."

"Did you just throw up?" I ask turning my face in the opposite direction.

"No, it was someone else, but... I have taken over this bench in particular. Nobody else will come near it because of that stinking puddle and that keeps me safe for a while. The sun and wind will dry it all up soon."

All this time the homeless man has not moved the morning newspaper from his face. I do not scare him. He speaks with the calmness of a man absorbed by his breathing but who might be simply half-awake to the day. Dressed in a bottle green coat, worn black sweatpants and a purple, woollen toque, he is in no hurry to start the day. Two stuffed green garbage bags might hold his possessions. One of the bags is bunched at his feet and the other he uses as a pillow. An empty shopping cart stands next to his right arm. Under his partially open coat, is a red and gray lined shirt and beneath the open necked shirt is a black t-shirt. His shoes are black and white running shoes that look fairly new. Good for him.

"I'll talk to you from under my newspaper because the sun is almost all up and is quite strong on the eyes. You wouldn't happen to have an extra pair of sunglasses on you… would you for a squinting old guy?" he asks.

I think of giving him my sunglasses but stop when I notice a pair partially sticking out of his coat pocket. A price tag from a convenience store is attached to an arm of the sunglasses. Doesn't the man realize what I can see? And those sunglasses look better than the ones I'm wearing.

"Since I see you already have a pair of sunglasses sticking out of your coat pocket, why do you need a second pair?"

"Oh!"

Then at almost the same time as he pushes the newspaper away from his face, the man quickly shoves the pilfered sunglasses into his coat pocket. To my shock, he's wearing another pair of sunglasses. "Are you in the sunglasses business?" I ask nudging my own sunglasses up my nose.

"Okay, it's my buddy who is also homeless like me. He sells sunglasses at the other end of the canal. We steal them from the stores and sometimes tourists who, you know, leave… them on the beach."

"Sure, I get it," I say. "But you can't have mine."

"Don't you have someplace to go?" the man says now sitting up on his bench. "Isn't that your bus?"

A tiny bird does a dance in the drying puddle, its claws already caked.

"See ya," I say.

Perfect

Two men with overflowing shopping carts stop at a bench, plop themselves down and absorb what the sun has to offer.

The younger of the two men has a black beard that springs out everywhere and threatens to take over his face. His blue eyes are alive, curious and he may be too tall to sleep on the bench. Wearing a faded brown ski jacket which opens to a solid green T-shirt underneath, his blue jeans are no longer blue. His coal black hair salutes the sky at different angles. When the man laughs, he giggles out of control as if his entire upper body were trying to get away from him. He looks at the much older man beside him and waits for the next funny story to spill from his lips.

The older man has, what might be, a week-old white beard sprouting from his face. Everything about this man is faded denim- his shirt, his open jacket, his jeans… even a beat-up denim cap. "I'm just about ready for my weekly shave," the older man says. "People give me more money if I'm clean-shaven. Go figure," he says.

"I don't care. I just panhandle with the face I have," the younger man replies.

"Well, my perfect face helped me have a few drinks last night and hook up with a woman under that walkway over the canal. I thought she was a real looker last night. When we woke up this morning, she smiled at me with a perfect mouth…one tooth at the bottom and one tooth at the top!"

The younger man stands. Then he points at the older man's mouth and his own mouth. Laughing and shaking and laughing and shaking, he holds his sides tightly, as if he were protecting his laughter from spilling into the canal.

"Be careful you don't fall into the water," the older man says while nudging his denim cap further back on his head. "Yeah, maybe we're all one-tooth wonders."

Finally, the younger guy slumps down on the bench exhausted from his laughing.

"But I shouldn't talk about perfect teeth because the four I have left are certainly not," the older man says pointing to his own greenish-yellow smile. "And I'm no looker myself! Besides, perfect teeth make me yawn."

The two men fall silent. A curious wind sweeps across their foreheads and then vanishes.

A young white couple jog by at precisely the same speed and everything about them matches and is new-their mid-blue jogging clothes, their blue and black runners… even the navy-coloured sweatbands on their foreheads and wrists. They smile the same flat smile at each other and at precisely the same time, as if both of their beings are entirely synchronized… a marvel in blue.

An elderly man wearing white designer sunglasses, a Tilly hat and a matching vest, short-sleeve shirt and khaki pants, walks by with his Golden Retriever. Above his huge grin is a white mustache so long and thick that it could nudge passersby into the canal. Both he and his dog almost march through the daylight to the beat of some silent, never-ending music. The dog's golden coat shimmers and shines and re-defines the word "exquisite". Bending over the dog, the man kisses the top of its head and says aloud: "Every bone is where it should be. You're a beauty!"

The younger man on the bench looks at the older guy beside and sighs, as if exhaling has its own language. Then their conversation becomes animated again because their arms and hands become a flurry of joy. Suddenly, the two men turn and face one another, then twist back towards the canal. Later they gesture at another small miracle on the canal and absorb what the sun has to offer.

Minding Business

"MIND YOUR OWN BUSINESS AND KISS YOUR OWN ASS!" THE MAN shouts at everyone waiting for a bus on the boulevard.

Eyes drop to the ground, as if searching for something. Their looking moves up and down from one side to the next. Feet shuffle, as if they are in the wrong shoes. Bags and purses shift from one hand to the other. Then everyone becomes frozen in place. The man, probably in his early twenties, is tall, slender and seems to be wired for anger. He wears torn beige shorts and a sleeveless, black T-shirt with the words "Take No Prisoners" emblazoned in red across the chest. His bare feet are scarred and smudged with streaks of dirt; if there is a difference between his dirt and his scars, it can't be seen.

A teenaged girl with short hair the color of oak, moves towards the screamer and thrusts her freckled face at him shouting: "Hey you, stop disturbing everyone! Leave us alone!" But the screamer flicks his right wrist at the girl's face, opens his mouth wide and grits his yellow teeth at her. "Like I said before, mind your own business and kiss your own butt," he says to the girl. "Or else."

"Or else what?" a tall African American woman says in a voice deeper than the canal. The screamer becomes silent as he watches the African American woman move to within an arm's length of the screamer's face.

People inhale sharply and even the strong winds blowing over the canal stop dead and plop into the water. Cars and trucks slow down and then speed up. Trollies and open busses stuffed with tourists pick up speed so that visitors don't get the wrong idea. Bikers and scooter drivers almost crash because their drivers are too curious when they pass by.

Finally, the African American woman points at the screamer and says," You are not in your own home here, so chill out and leave everyone alone!" And that does it. The screamer stops.

The bus arrives. Passengers file out. The driver senses trouble. He waits then gets up from his seat. After he exits his bus the driver takes a long look at the screamer.

"You…are not getting on my bus today! Got it? I can tell by these peoples' faces that you've been at it again. This is the third time this week. Get going before I call the cops. Everyone else, welcome aboard."

The screamer leaves quickly, soundlessly… on the tips of his toes.

Nearly everyone at the bus stop thanks the African American woman and wishes they had done like her. It turns out that the African American woman is not taking this particular bus and will wait, as she says, "for the next screamer." Passengers, filing onto the bus, laugh at the woman's joke. Some also throw up their hands at the sky and roll their eyes.

The sky breathes easier. Passersby see nothing but a solitary African American woman sitting on a bench, her right ankle resting on her left knee like a man might do and a face so calm it could float down the canal on its own and never blink. Even the occasional slight screeching of brakes punctuates the moment with reassuring order.

Minutes later, the African America woman's bus arrives. She uncrosses her right leg, stands, slowly shakes her head while smiling at nobody in particular and climbs aboard the bus. No one's left at the bus stop. On the bench is a forgotten brown lunch bag, its paper baking in the sun. Like a driverless bus, the canal floats by with its own passengers. Two tree leaves hanging beside each other are unsure if they should hide or applaud.

"Mind your own business and kiss your own ass."

Murky

Leaning will do that.

Standing on the lip of the canal, the short man wearing a pale green T-shirt and dark green shorts, stands up on the toes of his running shoes, almost leaning into the canal and studies the murky water.

"I can see right through that mucky water to the bottom," he says to me with assurance. "Even with my sunglasses on!"

"I can barely see below the surface with no sunglasses," I say. "Good for you."

"Thanks. I've had lots of experience under water. I also try to wear green clothes most of the time. Green is hope. Green is optimistic."

"Okay, but how did you get all that underwater experience?"

Meanwhile, the noonday sun is stronger than strong today, its heat baking my hair under my hat. The man beside me is still on his toes. He examines the canal water so carefully that I wonder if he is thinking of jumping in.

"Every time my parents took me to a public swimming pool, I used to dive to the bottom and hold my breath for as long as I could. When I came to the surface, I always hoped that my mother and father stopped shouting at each other."

Immediately, I imagine the man sitting patiently at the bottom of the canal holding his breath and I can see his puffy cheeks. His eyes bulge and plead. To my left the man's parents debate with one another about who is right and who is wrong, their wedding rings flashing hostility in the air. Soon the debate escalates and becomes a shouting match with both standing and holding hands on hips. They can't decide if each wants to be right or be happy.

Looking back into the canal, the man at the bottom has a face ready to explode. He is starting to thrash and should surface shortly. His parents, to my left, scream so loudly, the one cloud in the sky fades and then disappears. Their faces are rage-red. Other people walking or jogging by either give them a quick look or pretend the man and woman don't exist. Everyone gives the couple a wide berth. Bursting out of the water the man dressed in green trudges up the cement steps. I don't know if he's planning to heave both of his parents into the canal to rinse the madness from their bodies or simply grab both by the shoulders and shake them empty of their boiling blood. He may also be planning to simply walk away and shed his parents, like old skins.

"I can't imagine when my parents first became angry," he says.

Two grey-white clouds now cover the sun. Other clouds move herd-like towards where the sun's rays cook in their own heat. Drops of hesitant rain touch our faces. The man in green smiles so broadly that his right ear is introduced to his left ear.

"I'd rather be happy", he says as he jogs off to the bridge in the distance.

Leaning will do that.

Up To Here

Billy knows what's behind his name.

In his motorized wheelchair, a man in his fifties with a grey cardboard sign hanging from his neck, stops suddenly beside me and points to the name "Billy" printed on the sign.

"Hi Billy," I say.

Below us the canal waters flow smoothly as several paddle boats filled with women heave their way by us in a Dragon Boat Race. I can tell by their chants that they may be survivors from breast cancer or perhaps from some other serious disease. I love their determination and I imagine the cracked puzzle pieces of pain on their faces when they first found out about their illnesses.

"At least most of them will walk when they finish the race and climb out of those boats," Billy says. "It looks that way, anyhow."

"Hope so," I answer shifting from my right foot to my left and tugging my hat forward. "But you never know."

"I wonder what those women laugh about?"

Then Billy talks about how he lost his legs while on duty in Afghanistan.

"Nothing like those women in the boats with cancer, or at least I think so. I was working as a mechanic on a crew with three other men in an open field. We got attacked and both of my legs got hit. Just like that. Blood, bone, skin, everywhere. The other crew members scooped me up and hauled me back to shelter. Luckily the other men didn't have a scratch on them. Neither of my legs could be saved. And I didn't want those fake ones."

"How's life for you now?" I ask.

"Ah, I occasionally laugh about it but sometimes the joke is on me."

"What do you mean?"

"Well, I had this girlfriend who had legs that went on forever. Seriously, I'm not trying to be a smartass but I actually pursued her because of her legs but then found out she was brilliant and much more of an amazing person than I could ever be…even if I had her legs. She wore black leather boots up to here," Billy says pointing to his hip. "And she didn't mind me being in a wheelchair."

"How did you two get along?" I ask my head tilted to one side out of curiosity.

"Great…until she got pregnant. She said I was the father. Sure, we had some intriguing sex together but my doctor also said I had some nerve damage in my groin so I used Viagra. Sometimes I couldn't come so I don't know for sure if I'm the father. Ah, maybe I'm just too hard on myself."

"Why didn't you get your DNA tested?" I ask giggling at his last comment.

"I have a better idea. Let's go to the finish line of that Dragon Boat race. There's something I want to ask the winning team. Those intriguing women have something I want!"

The two of us race down to the end of the canal with Billy flying at top speed in his wheelchair. He arrives sooner than me.

Women soon hover over his wheel chair, their exuberance covering Billy, like a light summer rain. I hear Billy's laughter. I hear his wheelchair creaking. I hear myself wondering what's next.

Billy knows what's behind his name.

Was It Food?

TWO MEN WITH HEADS LIKE CIGAR ASH SIT ON A BENCH PLAYING CHESS while the canal water crawls by, like a movie from the 1940's. Each man puffs on a fat brown smoke and their exhaling becomes a waterfront mist in the same film. The first man is short, stout, has thick hair, like wool and his chins are too many to count. The second man has a crown of puffy cloud hair combed back tightly on the sides and he looks as if he has been the same size all his life.

Man One: "Remember that tall guy who caused such a racket at the meeting last week?"
Man Two: "Sure do. He just wouldn't shut up. He was friggin' nuts!"
Man One: "I had to call the police. It took four cops to get him into the back seat of the cruiser."
Man Two: "I heard that when they got him downtown, it took the same four cops to lock the guy up."
Man One: "None of the police wanted to go near that nutcase-even though he was locked up alone."
Man Two: "Yeah, but I heard later they had to feed the wacko and weren't sure how to do that." Man One: "So what did the cops do?"
Man One: "So what did the cops do?"
Man Two: "Well, it took them a while to figure it out. They first tried bringing him a spaghetti supper in one of those Styrofoam containers but the guy threw the meatballs and then the spaghetti everywhere and started ripping apart the Styrofoam with his teeth."

Man One: "Then what?"

Man Two: "Later, someone brought him a burger and fries in a paper bag and he kicked the burger around the cage, while flicking the fries, one by one, through the bars at passing policeman. Imagine, shortly after that, the same guy complained that he was hungry and had a right to be fed."

Man One: "That's insane."

Man Two: "I know but sooner or later, the guy had to eat. The police officers in the office were now hesitant to even walk by the cell."

Man One: "So what did they do?"

Man Two: "Someone in charge dug into one of drawers of his desk and pulled out a huge slingshot. He carefully laid the slingshot on his desk and said he'd be back shortly."

Man One: "So where did the man in charge go?"

Man Two: "Out to pick up something for the madman."

Man One: "Was it for food?"

Man Two: "Actually, it was a bag of tiny bananas."

Man One: "Bananas? I don't get it."

Man Two: "The cop in charge said those bananas are tasty. Then, he picked up the slingshot, and aimed carefully at the cell. Sometimes, the bananas zipped straight through the bars either hitting the crazy guy or the walls. Often, a banana wouldn't make it. About twenty bananas later, the man in charge dropped the slingshot into a bottom drawer of his desk."

Man One: (now laughing so hard and choking on his cigar): "Did the small bananas get eaten?"

Man Two: "Yes and not a single one was thrown back or squished on the floor or on the walls of the cell. Must have hit a sweet spot."

Man One: "But what's so special about tiny bananas?"

Man Two: "Maybe it's because they're firm, sweet and don't bleed like spaghetti sauce."

And their chess game remains untouched because this 1940's film never ends.

Right Thing

WHO IS DOING THE LISTENING HERE?

Two men stand straight up to the sky at the top of the canal watching the water ebb by. The taller of the two is trying to add up the dollar bills in his wallet. The second man, who is a head shorter, wants his taller friend to stop the money counting and listen only to him.

"Can't you see that I'm trying to count my cash," the taller man says. "Hang on, will you."

The shorter man knows that in his airline supply job, he should never be placed in charge of people because he is too fussy. It's always the same. Co-workers say he drives them crazy.

"Listen to me and stop worrying about your wallet!" he tells the taller man.

"Okay. Okay."

"I'm often told that I am one of the best workers they've ever had. I'm always on time. Keep great records. I'm not lazy. I work harder than anyone. But… they let me go because of complaints from my co-workers. Imagine, after all those compliments, they fired me this morning."

The taller man has finished counting his dollars and tucks his wallet into his back pocket. Then he turns to the shorter man and looks him in the eye.

"Are you sure you didn't do anything else or forget to do something at work?"

"Not really. For example, I don't steal like many others do. You should see…people grab everything from toilet paper to bottled water. Cases of the stuff are taken all the time."

"How do they get away with that?" the taller man asks. "Doesn't the airline ever check? What about security?"

"Oh, the airline has security at the airport itself but not in the warehouse where all the supplies are stored. That's where I worked." explains the shorter man.

"Maybe your co-workers got together and reported you for being too nit-picky."

"Tough! Don't most employers want workers to be finicky?"

"Probably but sometimes you push people too far, like you did before when I was trying to count my money."

"I just wanted you to listen to me, like I did with my co-workers. What's wrong with that?"

"Unfortunately, not everything is about you…or me… for that matter."

Over the canal, there is a humming factory sound in the bright afternoon. Two teenage boys at opposite sides of the water try to fling small rubber balls to each other across the canal, like an impossible pitch and catch game. The balls simply drop in the water far before they reach their intended targets.

"Did you ever report anyone for stealing?" the taller man asks after smiling at the efforts of the teenagers.

"Only once but I was really careful about it," the shorter man says, his words measured, like cuffs on new pants.

"However, in an odd way, you were also taking money out of your co-workers pockets because they now have to buy their own toilet paper and bottled water."

"Well… at least I didn't steal and I did the right thing."

"Yeah, but it's done and over with so it's time to move on," says the taller man patting his wallet in his back pocket.

Who is doing the listening here?

I Need More Maturing

THE WEIGHT-LIFTER, WHO MAY HAVE BEEN BORN WITH AN ALL-TEETH smile, was probably raised in a skin-tight T-shirt. He puffs out his chest on that canvas of an afternoon. Sitting on the canal wall, the man tilts his face upwards, snorts the contents of his nose back into his head twice and says, "You know what… you know what, I think that women may have gone too far," as if he is still frozen in the 1950's.

There is nobody near the weight- lifter except for one person directly behind him on a bench and hiding behind a newspaper. The man of weights talks silently to the canal, to the birds, to the trees, and to the sun perched on a cloud. He could also be sitting on the edge of a table at the back of a church hall at a Saturday night, teenage dance. He won't ask girls to dance. Instead, he remains perched in his T-shirt, his balloon chest expecting everyone to notice him.

"I want the girls to come to me," he might be saying to himself.

Perhaps he spent the afternoon lying in the sunlight making sure his face was burnt just enough to put himself on display at the dance or… on the canal wall. Yeah, look at him, look at him.

"For a guy of sixty-five, women tell me I need more maturing," he mutters. "Yeah, I want to grow up but I don't know what that looks like or how to do it. A friend once suggested that maybe my pride was holding me back but screw him!"

What does the weight-lifter lack? Does he lack humility, self-restraint, experience, wisdom, perfection, skills, cultivation, sophistication, poise or is he not settled enough? All this judging reminds me of suddenly opening a window and the wind blowing everything away.

Perhaps he never felt good enough for the father of his very first girlfriend. The father, who was a medical doctor, didn't like the working-class look of his daughter's boyfriend. Still, the boy kept seeing the doctor's daughter and began sticking out his chest to protect himself from the doctor's downward glances. Eventually, he broke off with his heartbroken daughter to remind her father that she was no longer… good enough for him.

Later, while the weight-lifter stares across the canal, a pigeon shits on the back of his T-shirt. "Damn bird!" he shouts.

The weight-lifter grabs the nearest trash basket and dumps it on the pathway. Then he picks up a few empty bottles and any other trash and flings everything at the bird which takes off and gleefully slashes at the sky with its own weightless song. Finally, flinging the empty trash basket into the canal, the man then wipes his back against a tree trunk. Soon he is down on his hands doing push-up after push-up until another pigeon lands a couple of arm lengths away from him. Spotting the bird out of the corner of his eye, the man suddenly lunges and grabs the pigeon by its throat. He stands quickly, squeezes hard, spins the bird's body, like a small plastic bag of produce, while holding its neck and then flings the dead bird into the middle of the canal.

"You… are… a piece of crap!" he yells at the dead pigeon now sinking to the bottom of the canal. The weight-lifter then climbs down the steps leading to the canal, dips both hands into the water, shakes away the feathered death from his fingers and then wipes his hands on the legs of his jeans, as if no pigeon deserves a life of its own. Removing his T-shirt, he rinses it in the canal making sure the bird droppings have been washed away. Back up the steps he goes with his wet T-shirt in hand and then parks himself again on the canal wall. His T-shirt is spread out beside him in the sunlight and his bare chest heaves in and out and in and out, his rage as raw as a haunting childhood memory.

Decisions

HOW DID HE DECIDE?

The man on the bench next to the boathouse can't decide if he will take his third wife to a family gathering in a faraway city.

His hair has probably been dyed black so often that it now looks reddish in colour on top of a face mapped with lines upon lines… family lines coloured in memories.

"I'm not crazy about flying and there are so many messed up heads in my family. I'm not sure if we'll go. You know how it can be with family and I've run out of buttons to be pushed Yet, I'd look forward to getting out of here because I get cabin fever and need to get away."

The manager of the boathouse, who might be a few years older, has been lending his ear to all this talk.

"You sound a lot like my own father," the boat house manager finally says while scratching his right ear. "He's working on his third marriage too."

This morning the heat hangs fever-like over the canal. There's not a hint of wind anywhere. Pedestrians walk by with careful steps while sipping from plastic water bottles. Even a overstuffed bulldog drips sweat as it waddles with its owner along the pathway near the boat house. Above the canal, the sun screams its heat at the day. Canal walls are oven walls.

Then the man with the reddish-black hair, continues:

"You know, one of my sons from my first marriage is about your age," he tells the boathouse manager. "He's exactly like me. Same fears. Same anger. Refuses to talk to me! Then, there's my youngest daughter from my second wife and she's terrified of me. Other kids from both of my past marriages pretend I don't exist. Each of my ex-wives, now re-married, was and probably still is, an incredible person…intelligent…articulate…kind…even tough and I almost killed them both. Now I'm supposed to attend this family reunion. Might be safer to hide in a zoo."

"Didn't you tell me the other day that you've done a lot of work on yourself?" the boathouse manager asks. "That's not what your face says right now."

"You know what? It's too hot today to make any decisions. Think I'll go for a walk and let the canal decide."

"How will that work?"

"Well, this waterway must be several miles long and a lot of rivers and streams flow into it, a lot of possibilities, before it all runs into some big body of water. This canal's been around for many decades and has probably seen and heard it all."

"But the water is lifeless, especially today.".

"Perhaps that stillness is just what I need. I better go."

Walking away from the boathouse, the man with the reddish-black hair is almost swallowed by the walls of heat. Suddenly, he stops, points his right index finger upwards, salutes both the sky and the canal, studies his fingers, and lying there in the palm of his hand is another canal marvel…a "do nothing" solution.

How did he decide?

The Whiteness

THE MAN IN HIS GARDEN IS A MAN OF WHITE.

His longish hair, partially covered by a cloud-coloured floppy hat, could be freshly fallen snow while his droopy mustache is as white as chalk. Dressed in a white T-shirt and white khaki pants rolled up above his ankles and sandals, the man looks as if he bathed in milk this morning.

As he sits, he curls his legs under him on a wooden bench meant only for two people. The man's plot is barren, flat. What does he grow here? No garden tools. No pots. No wires or overhead string or rope. Nothing but him and his small bench. Perhaps he uses the community hoses only to quench his thirst or to wash the dust from his bench. The man's eyes actually open wider and wider as they follow the canal current all the way to that big body of water elsewhere. His eyes go far enough to get lost.

A young jogger, pushing her child in a carriage, doesn't break her stride, and gives the garden man a tiny wave as she passes by. In a measured response, he nods at her and continues eyeing the canal. Three women tourists stop by the man's garden and point at the emptiness. One of the women tries to engage the garden man in a conversation with lots of hand waving but he remains silent and returns a measured smile. The second woman holds her i-phone in the air, as if asking the man if she could take his picture. He agrees and she snaps twice on her phone. Then the same woman gestures at the man asking him if she might enter his garden and take a "selfie" of with him and her. Shaking his head, he holds up both hands and she gets it. The third woman begins tugging her two friends away. After bowing and more bowing, like silent hinges, the three women leave.

Two teenage boys carrying their treasured skateboards under their arms stop at the man in white and are frozen by their own curiosity. The taller of the two boys shifts his skateboard from his left arm to his right arm and back again. Dropping his skateboard to the ground, the second boy wheels his board back and forth with his right foot without looking.

"There's nothing growing in that man's garden!" the taller boy announces loudly.

"Maybe not right now," the other boy says. "But it must be that way for a reason."

"I'll ask him," says the taller boy who leans close to the wired fence.

"What's in your garden?"

"Just enough," the white-haired man answers.

"What do you mean?"

The man in white says nothing.

"What do you mean?" the taller boy asks again.

"I've already answered."

"Let's leave him alone," the shorter boy says as he pulls his taller friend away from the fence. Taking their curiosity with them, like a backpack, the boys leave.

The garden man in white uncurls his legs, stands and moves to the wired fence closest to the canal. After examining the canal's current, he exhales in the slowest of motions and then gives a deliberate wink at the soil beneath his feet.

Five Orange Pylons and a Red Scooter

In the hesitant mid-morning light, the water is momentarily clear.

Five orange pylons and a rusted, red children's scooter sit at the bottom. Each pylon stands perfectly tall, like part of an underwater obstacle course. However, fish of all sizes appear to twist and weave their way through their own invisible course and ignore the pylons. Do the fish know better?

Perhaps a boy threw both pylons and scooter into the canal after losing a competition. Yes, there he is pushing his scooter around each pylon gasping and heaving his way to the finish line. Other contestants fly by the boy so he pushes himself harder. At the end, several other racers wait for the boy to complete the course and he comes in last. Putting on a brave face, he realizes that everyone has completed the race before him. Then the boy mutters to himself, throws his scooter on the grass and sits under a tree with his arms folded, a "leave me alone" look. One by one, the other racers try to console him but the boy's bottom lip is a wall so they leave him alone. Before the other racers collect their scooters and head home, one of them asks the boy to collect the pylons.

"Later," he says. "Yeah, sure I'll do it.

After he has gathered up the five pylons, he waits until everyone is gone before flinging each one into the canal where they settle down almost in a perfect circle. Then the boy grabs his red scooter by the handlebar and heaves it high into the air. The scooter splashes down on top of the underwater pylons and slowly sinks to the bottom.

"If I don't win, nobody wins" the boy shouts at the sky. "Nobody!"

The scooter settles among the murky pylons. A thin, dark eel hesitates and then slithers around the front wheel of the scooter. Most other underwater life stays away from the pylons and scooter until the water is calm again.

Maybe the boy thinks about jumping into the canal to retrieve the pylons and scooter but stops right there after removing his sandals. The water is filthy, toxic. He's heard of a man jumping in after a dropped wallet and dying of septic shock. No, the scooter and pylons can be replaced. The boy's face is resigned. Even a loser eventually wants to keep living. When he looks into the canal again, he now sees swarms of creatures curling in and around the pylons. They leave the scooter untouched for the moment, as if the toy were a trophy ready to be claimed only later. The pylons swerve. The water becomes more cloudy. Other fish scatter, as if exploding from a magician's wand.

The two largest eels swarm around the scooter and actually ride it underwater westward towards a destination in an act of pure, frantic beauty. There are no other racers underwater and the eels ride the scooter, as if their lives depended on the outcome. The boy's eyes follow the eels for as long as possible. Then he turns and looks at the pylons, the sun making them flaming cones.

After stepping back from the canal, the boy shuffles over the path and drops himself down on a bench. He looks to the left, to the right and back again. Then a smile, as wide as a finish line, lifts his face in victory, as if winners and losers were a common phenomenon on the canal.

In the hesitant, mid-morning light, the water is momentarily clear.

White-Out

There the hidden cloud sits.

In the middle of a garden stacked with flower-pots, wood, plastic and rusted folding chairs sits a tiny plot of soil where the leaves seem to give birth to tiny suns. Set in the centre of confusion and protected by walls of clutter, this soil is full of questions.

Directly outside this walled-in life, an African-American man talks in a strong, clear voice. He sounds as if he's rehearsing for something or someone because he gestures at the canal and to the person sitting beside him and there is only one other person on the bench - a patient friend of his, also an African American man.

"Not trying to sound too clever" he says to his friend. "But I had my first white-out on my sixteenth birthday party after drinking way too much vodka and I promptly forgot the first sixteen years of my life. I certainly can't call it a 'black-out' because seriously, my brain was filled with nothing but the whitest of foams at the time. Because I haven't had any booze since, I don't believe I have a drinking problem. Yet, how does anyone forget sixteen years?"

The garden disarray is unmoved by the man's words. Only the leaves of that tiny plant have folded inward, as if they were absorbing what he said and are beginning the hunt for the lost time. Where are those years?

The leaves might be curious ears imagining the man's boyhood, especially the formative years. "During those first years at home, my mother encouraged me to go play outside and shortly after she'd say: 'All you ever do is think of yourself and going outside to play!' My father's moods changed from encouraging me to read as many great books as possible to saying: 'You think you're smarter than everyone because you read so many books? Well, have I got news for you!'"

Maybe these comments had something to do with those lost years, like a memory puzzle lacking pieces.

The African American man looks straight at his friend and motions for the friend to sit closer. "So, what do you think happened?" he asks. "And how do I get those years back?"

"I'm more curious about that white foam," the friend says. "What is that and where did it come from?"

"Not sure. However, I was surrounded by white kids when I was a boy. My teachers were mostly white. Most years I was the only Black kid in class or in the neighbourhood but I seldom felt out of place. I didn't get teased that much. One time a kid made a crack about the size of my head so after school I introduced his testicles to his nostrils with my foot."

"Listen to yourself, "the friend says. "The years are coming back. They matter."

"Yeah, they do," the man replies.

"What else do you recall?"

"I'll have to let you know when that foam is loses its bubbles… at my feet," as if all spills showed a lack of ambiguity.

There the hidden cloud sits.

Maybe

"LIKE ALL MY MAYBE'S", HE SAYS.

The red-headed man tells me he's originally from Tulsa, Oklahoma and works as a caretaker in an apartment building not far from the canal. He used to write songs and sing in bars in Tulsa and closed those same bars down more often than not.

"I no longer drink or sing and am now married to a woman from Osaka," he tells me.

The woman, in her early fifties, loves to run in marathons and has the wiry frame of a twelve-year-old. However, whenever she opens her mouth, she starts with: "Why is everyone so hard on me?"

"In Japan", she tells him, "I worked as a pharmacist but why can't I find the same work here?" Several times she has taken English language proficiency tests to become a pharmacist but failed simply because her English wasn't strong enough.

"The test is too hard for anyone," the caretaker tells me.

Yesterday, the same man sat next to me again on a bench along the canal.

"I had to drive my moped all the way to Chinatown in the pouring rain just to pick up a phone battery for a renter. What a pain!"

The caretaker makes sure that anyone who passed by heard how horrible it was to drive through the light July rain for a phone battery. Finally, a woman passing by stops and tells him that he is carrying quite a load on his shoulders.

"Yes," he replies. "That phone battery was very expensive and quite a burden."

"What are you doing…carrying around a cross or something" the woman asks.

The caretaker's mouth drops open and I'm laughing so hard I nearly tumble off the bench.

"Everyone cries POOR, including me sometimes", I hear the woman say as she slowly moves away from us.

"Me too," I add wiping a laughter tear from my cheek.

Later I discover that the caretaker's financial portfolio is huge and he is planning to buy a second condo.

"Part of my work deal is that we live in a rent-free apartment. We have a moped, a car, a paid in pull condo that I rent out, and a bunch of money invested."

"Ever thought of investing in more English courses for your wife?" I ask.

"I have done that. It is possible that her English is as good as it's going to get. Perhaps she can try for other jobs, like being a tourist guide."

"Yeah, all those "could be's" makes it hard to know for sure," I say. "Sorry if I laughed earlier." "Nah, it's okay," the caretaker says waving his right hand dismissively at me.

"Do you ever actually think you're carrying around too much of a burden?" I ask.

"Maybe. Does that ever happen to you?"

"Only when my bottom lip sags."

"How often does that happen?" he asks.

"It seems to sag when the moment's just right…or just wrong."

"Like all my maybe's," he says.

Discussion

AT NIGHT THE PEBBLES TOO MAY QUIETLY TURN OVER IN THE COOL darkness and use the moon as their blanket.

Two men sit on an early morning bench and discuss how they regularly go to the rear of a 7-Eleven store at midnight when unsold sandwiches are being discarded.

"That's where I get my main meal of the day," the first man says yawning at the bright sky. In his mid-fifties, he has hair the colour of tree bark and a face that is filled with ruts, as if life for him were a series of blows from an axe. He wears a faded black wind-breaker that is zipped up to his chin and colourless jeans with worn-out knees. On his head is a fairly new red and black baseball cap and on his feet are flip-flop sandals that threaten to fall apart with his next step.

"Yeah, thank goodness for 7-Eleven," he says.

The second man, closer to seventy than sixty, wears a long, grey, cloth coat completely opened to the comforting sun. Above each of his ears is a fringe of white hair. He is dressed in a light blue denim shirt, tattered black jeans and a pair of purple and white running shoes with toes ready to explode.

"I like the way that 7-Eleven guy knows we're coming and already has those sandwiches ready for us in two bags," he says to the other man. "Often he also includes a coffee."

"Hope he's there tonight," the first man says. "He reminds me of something magic sprouting up between stones."

Across from the two men, an empty garden with a floor covered entirely with bone-white pebbles, listens to the discussion, like a giant corrugated ear. The stones seem to have no expectations. Perhaps the pebbles simply wait to learn when they will return to dust. In that barren garden, the white stones seem lifeless but are actually shaping their own language like the kind words of that 7-Eleven clerk. Before even falling asleep, the two homeless men turn sideways and study the garden floor and are assured by the thought of possible food... somewhere.

The men plan their day carefully, which includes several hours of safe sleep in the sunshine. They intend to sleep close by each other on separate benches.

"The day is safe. The night is not," the younger man says. "During the darkness, we keep moving, as if night were day.

"Not much interests me during the day anyway," the older man says. "And it's past my bedtime. See you later."

"Right," the younger man says. "Time to shut my face."

Each man takes over his bench. Faces are covered, one with a small green towel and the other with a 7-Eleven plastic bag. Legs are pulled upward and each faces the back of his own bench. The younger man pulls a light blue tarp over himself while the older one buttons up his long, grey coat to his neck, like the giant, dusty leaves of a plant. At the end of each bench are their Safeway carts filled with real and imagined necessities.

At night the pebbles too may quietly turn over in the cool darkness and use the moon as their blanket.

What Do You Hear Right Now?

"I'M PROUD TO HAVE LASTED THIS LONG," A MAN WITH FLOUR-WHITE hair says as he plumps down on my bench.

"Pardon me?" I say looking up from my paperback novel.

"I'm satisfied to have lived this long and for being an expert on silence."

I wish that he would just leave me and my book alone. Doesn't he get my need for quiet?

I notice that he wears a long-sleeved white shirt, khaki vest and matching pants. His dark brown walking shoes look as if they've seen better days. Perhaps he is a recent retiree from somewhere.

"I come from an Iowa farm family," he says and that makes me close my book because I come from a place of apartment buildings, smokestacks, train tracks and factories.

"I know little about farm life," I reply.

"Okay. Let's start with our farmhouse. That was the place my father had people over to party. He'd come back from town with his truck filled with people and another truck behind him. That was when my mother took off with our car for a winding drive in the fields."

"But what about all those long hours I've heard it takes to run a farm?"

"I'm not sure. I left as soon as I could. My father was a great starter of tasks but very few jobs got finished. No matter how hard he tried to fix something, it was always broken."

"What happened with all those people at your place and what did you do?" I ask.

"I'm not sure what they were doing but they were noisy. Mom told us to hide under our beds or in closets because we were expected to behave…at all times."

"When did you eat?"

"We didn't. We were afraid. We waited for the partying to end. We were quiet," he says.

"What about your mother?" I ask, my curiosity growing.

"As we grew older, I found out that she would sit in the car and wait until everyone left. When my mother came into the house, the shouting began. After when we heard the front door slam, we knew my father was gone for the night and it was then we all came out from hiding. Time to eat."

I listen for the quiet but there is none. Men and women walk by chatting to each other in the easy daylight. A boy struts by carrying a skateboard under his left arm and he can be heard spinning its wheels with his right hand. Joggers bob by, their shoes thumping on the path. People in a large passing canoe are encouraged by a single voice to paddle in unison. Vehicles on the boulevard running next to the canal make their moped, car, truck and bus noises one after the other, like a background scene from a TV show. In the distance, looking southward, patient jet planes slice through the sky and begin their descent to the airport. Birds screech above us, as if they are trying to shock a cloud out of the sky.

"Did your mother or father ever actually tell you… to be quiet?" I ask.

"Nope. Not once. We just knew. That was our farm life. It made me an expert on peace and quiet. And…I'm proud to have lasted this long."

Leftovers

THE HOMELESS MAN IS CONTEMPLATING...SOMETHING.

Leaning on the handlebar of his shopping cart, he may be thinking of breakfast as I walk briskly towards him during my morning workout. From inside his cart, he retrieves a large Styrofoam container which he lifts to the top of his heap and lays it there. Prying open the container in the morning light, a small portion of leftover spaghetti with two meatballs pops out in the sun. From the bottom of his shopping cart, he pulls out a small black cardboard box containing several tiny glass bottles - his own spice rack. A long white plastic fork appears from his inside jacket pocket which he thrusts into a meatball. From each small glass bottle, he sprinkles what looks like salt, pepper and maybe garlic powder on his food. Then, he tucks a napkin into the collar of his shirt and starts eating.

"Good morning," I say stopping about two feet from the man and his shopping cart.

"Good morning to you too," replies the man after chewing and swallowing some spaghetti and then laying his plastic fork on his meal. "Beautiful day."

"Yes, it is. Sorry if I'm interrupting your breakfast. Looks tasty."

"It is. Actually, I'm grateful to have anything to eat. Someone left this on a bench."

"Is the canal life your life?" I ask.

"Yes. I still sometimes get money from my deceased father's trust account. It's not enough to live on but it helps. My lawyer brother, who lives in a faraway city, manages the money.

I never take it for granted. When I'm really broke, I call my brother collect. However, I try not to call him much because he makes me feel small."

"What do you mean?"

"When I do call him, he's annoyed and sounds like he's doing me a huge favour. Like a forgotten toy under his boyhood bed… that's how he makes me feel. And he wouldn't know leftovers if they were dropped on his head or down his pants.

"Has he ever come here?"

"Nope, and I haven't seen him in a long time. I invited him to come a few years back but he'd heard of the summer crowds and he hates large groups."

"Too bad," I say plucking my sweaty T-shirt away from my chest.

"I love being near the canal," the homeless man replies. "Why bother travelling?"

I watch the man become taller as he stands and talks excitedly about the different people he meets.

"Mind if I finish eating?" he asks.

No, please, go ahead," I say.

Between mouthfuls of spaghetti, the man gradually becomes almost as tall as the lowest branch on the tree standing behind him. His delight is contagious and I too stand taller than normal, my shoulders as far back as they can go with little effort. Soon he tells me about people that he met yesterday.

"Yeah, this family, I think from South America, who spoke some English, were sitting on the wall of the canal and the father was reading a paperback novel. The water level was slowly rising but nobody told the father and both he and his book got soaked by a canal wave. Well, the rest of the family laughed so hard, as if they had just invented the beauty of rejoicing.

The homeless man is contemplating…something.

What Looks Like

THE WEALTHY MAN, MOVES WITH MEASURED STEPS ALONG THE PATH and stops to tie a shoelace on his "just off the shelf", all-leather walking shoes. Breathing like a Buddha and smiling like one too, he looks up at me and asks what I think of his shoes.

"Mighty classy," I answer surprised as men don't usually ask about shoes. "Never seen anything like them."

"Thanks," the man says. "Not to sound like I'm bragging, but my wife and I have finally decided to spend all our money so we buy Rolex watches to match our fancy shirts. But really, we're not braggarts!"

"Sure, I get it. You and your wife must be doing well."

"It wasn't always that way. We also have nine different cars back in Anaheim, California."

"Are you satisfied?"

"Maybe a little. I'm not sure what makes us happy," I say.

The gold rings on his fingers flash in the sun, as if money were meant for nothing but spending or brightness. All of this display of wealth doesn't seem like an act of showing off because he is not a trumpet and I hear sadness at the bottom of his voice.

"For several years, my wife and I thought of hiring a hit-man to kill our only son because the boy had become a ruthless, crooked drug dealer and user. We had tried everything including: kicking him out, ten treatment centres, having his blood drained and replaced in a Swiss clinic, psychiatrists, even hypnosis and having him locked up. Nothing worked. Nothing! And all of this didn't matter because after seventeen years of trying to help him, my son died from a bullet to the head and a drug overdose- both at the same time."

"Did someone shoot him or did he do it himself?" I ask.

"Doesn't matter. There was always someone out to get him. Maybe the person who killed him made it look like a suicide," the man replies, his shoulders dipping, unsure.

I can't imagine a mother and father hiring someone to murder their only son. However, eventually the emotional investment account is drained. What's next? Hire a hitman? Buy watches to match shirts?

The man keeps his eyes directly on mine. His jewellery and clothes could belong on a mannequin behind a high-end store window.

"What else could you do?" I ask.

After standing back, the man shakes and shudders and tears river down his face. His weeping shines more in the sun than the gold on his fingers and wrist. For a brief moment, I notice that the sky is unsure about this sorrow. Small fast-moving clouds momentarily cover the sun and then quickly move on, winds trying to even things out. I stand back because I am like a full-sized, hiding sun on a partially cloudy day… hesitant, assured, and then uncertain again. Why don't I just walk away from his heaving sadness?

"Have we met before?" he asks wiping his face dry with the back of his hand.

"I don't think so," I reply stepping away even further.

"Are you sure about that?" he asks again checking his Rolex, the ticking louder and louder on his left wrist.

Fist Face

"THANKS FOR LISTENING," HE ADDS. "AS OF NOW, MY PLAN FOR today is to look for normal."

On the canal bridge a wiry man strolling ahead of me, suddenly stops and asks for the time. After I tell him it is nine a.m., he half-smiles at me and his face almost cracks open, as if it has been hardened by fists of all sorts. "Don't I know you?" he asks.

"I don't think so," I reply with the hairs standing up on my neck.

"Can I bend your ear anyway?" he asks.

Sure I say "sure" because his face is made for my curiosity.

"I know this is awfully sudden. Hope you don't mind but... I gotta talk."

"Go ahead," I say.

"For many years as a boy I was taunted by others for being half-First Nations. They wouldn't stop until one day I grabbed the biggest guy and punched him so hard that a couple of his teeth spurted out of his bloodied mouth. After that I kept punching anyone who insulted me until the put-downs stopped. Today, I don't have to punch as much anymore because I just give people a hard stare. Last time I hammered someone in the mouth was many months ago.

"You're not gonna chop me up, are you?" a smart-assed guy said to me in a convenience store at the time. Well, I hit the guy so hard that a piece of his tooth got stuck in my knuckle. Doctors had me hooked up to an IV because I had an infection. Red stripes were running up and down my left arm.

Lucky for me they didn't have to amputate my arm."

My brain whispers: "What's his face going to tell me next?"

He sounds like that same man the police picked up last week. One of the cops told the media that this guy thought hostility was as normal as sitting on a toilet. At a family barbeque he promised to go home, get his gun and come back to shoot everyone who disagreed with him. But he never returned to the barbeque. Someone phoned the police anyway, gave them the man's address and he was taken downtown for his gun-threating behaviour. The story was reported in the media.

I wonder if some people passing us by on the bridge might recognize him from the newspaper because most of them give us a wide berth.

A woman jogger of about twenty, with short hair the colour of red brick and wearing a purple jogging outfit, stops suddenly, takes a second look at Fist Face and then runs off at double her speed.

Two men holding hands, perhaps in their mid-thirties, see us talking together and slow down their walking. Then they turn suddenly and walk back in the opposite direction, as if their lives were at risk.

A middle-aged woman, with short, caramel-coloured hair, moves steadily across the bridge. She stops and pretends to look over the canal and takes a quick glance in our direction, as if she isn't entirely sure where she saw Fist Face before today.

A tall, angular teenage boy with a shaved head and chains hanging from everywhere, pedals by, gives us a long stare, veers off the path towards the boulevard and almost slams into what looks like a brand-new Toyota Corolla filled with a family of four.

"I know what abnormal is and I think I'm all talked out," Fist Face finally says to me.

"Thanks for listening," he adds. "As of now, my plan for today is to look for normal."

Wheelchair

If only the man with the shaved head, could sit, long enough on the bench.

Midway down the canal, a middle-aged man waits patiently beside what could be his unconscious and perhaps terminally ill father who is slumped in a wheelchair. Grinding his teeth at the uneven summer sky, the man's face slips into a quick knot. Is he angry or is he nervous about his father? Will he push the wheelchair across the path and let it roll straight into the canal or… will he check to see if the wheelchair brake is still holding?

Perhaps the son was persuaded by his mother to finally spend some time with his dad. Their father-son relationship was mostly spent trying to fix something that couldn't be fixed.

Weak, he may recall how he saw his father as being weak. The son saw himself as either having no weaknesses or too many and only focussed on his father's lack of firmness and character.

It all happened one long ago day when his father, a retired railway traffic clerk, told him that he should think of going to secretarial school if he can't decide what to do in life. At the time, the young man could not believe that his father had such a lack of ambition.

"I don't know what I want to do in life but I certainly can't see myself as a clerk or secretary. There has to be something else but I don't know what that is."

"What's wrong with being a clerk or secretary? Start small and then move up from there," his dad had said.

"That's someone else's job," the young man replied.

"Easy does it, Son. Jobs are changing."

"Bullshit!"

"Why are you always so angry?" the father asked. "What's the matter?"

"I don't want what you have!"

"What?"

In the past, the father's eyes slid into another dimension of gloom while confusion contorted his face. Why was his son so difficult to get along with? Was it because this boy was the forgotten middle child? His older sister and younger brother seemed to be reasonably well-adjusted…whatever that meant.

"You are so naïve. You get taken in by salespeople. Remember that slick salesman who said you could have that silverware for free if… you could get eight people to display it in their homes in thirty days? However, if you didn't get eight people, you'd have to pay for the silverware yourself. That was a pyramid scam and you fell for it! And then your older brother, Uncle Ted, would have lunch with you and come back to your office so he could tell you how to do your job. He was a tax man and worked for the federal government. Your traffic clerk job was none of his business."

"He was my older brother and he just needed to be a big shot at the time. So I pretended to listen to him. Sometimes it's best to pretend."

"I don't want to make believe!" the son shouted back at his father.

Now, on a bench overlooking the canal, the son wraps his left arm around his father, adjusts the small dark blanket on his shoulders and checks the brake on the wheelchair.

If only his dad could go through the motions one more time.

If only the canal would stop flowing.

If only the man with the shaved head, could sit, long enough on the bench.

Limits

WHERE DOES ALL THIS COME FROM?

On a bridge overlapping the canal, I look over to my left and suddenly a compact rental car containing a young Asian couple, perhaps tourists, slams into a taxi driven by a local. It is mid-morning and the traffic is light. The road is dry. Sliding out of his vehicle, the cab driver approaches the rental car. He taps on the window and the Asian man rolls down his window. The cabbie motions to the driver to come out of the car and points to his own licence and insurance forms. As the Asian man gets out of his rented vehicle, he pulls out his wallet and shows the taxi-driver his license and insurance slip. Then he reaches back into the car and presents a form containing the rental registration information. The Asian driver struggles with his English. The other driver stumbles in broken English thinking his simplicity will help.

Soon the cab driver pulls out his cellphone and contacts the police. Because life here can be slow and easy, I am surprised a police cruiser arrived within minutes.

After writing his report, the local police officer calls for a tow-truck as the rear end of the cab is a mess. The other driver's rental has considerable front-end damage too.

The driver tries so hard to communicate but his words trip over his tongue and lips, like lost teeth. Speaking a fair amount of that Asian tongue, the police officer is able to get through to the driver. Questions are asked. Notes are taken. The Asian driver appears to feel some short-lived relief as he gestures while possibly telling the policeman that he took his eyes off the road. There is so much disgrace on the driver's face that one eye is filled with shame and the other guilt. Where does all that this come from? Does he hate himself? What's his secret? The Asian driver shuffles over to the curb and carefully sits down on the cold cement sidewalk. As he twirls both of his index fingers in the air, he creates two identical spirals of liability, as if he wants everyone to witness his descent into further remorse.

Meanwhile, his woman partner is at a loss as to what to do next. She sits down beside him on the curb and wrings her hands above her thighs. Then she touches her partner's left shoulder. He suddenly looks at her and shouts something causing her to immediately remove her right hand from his shoulder. After more hand-wringing, she stands and moves away from him and, if her shoulders were hunched any further, they would touch each other.

The police officer calls for a second tow-truck and then motions to both drivers to come with him to his vehicle and the taxi driver slides into the back seat while the Asian couple waits outside the police car. Meanwhile, the taxi-driver has an easy smile on his face as he knows he cannot be blamed.

"My lower back feels like wood, but I'll be fine," he can be heard telling the police officer.

"Better get checked out by a doctor anyway," the police officer replies. "You never know." "Sure. How's the driver? Both he and his wife look like corpses," the cabbie says.

"Maybe he's discovered his limits."

"Oh?"

"Sometimes drivers feel so terrible in an accident, even when they are not at fault. But it looks like he will be responsible because he slammed into the back of your cab. We'll have to keep an eye on him. I've seen that statue look before. Maybe his limits are quite different than yours or mine."

Where does all this come from?

What the Rain Does

THE EARLY MORNING SKY OVER THE CANAL IS GREY LIKE CHARCOAL woollen sweaters piled high on a shelf. I know this is temporary as the sun usually burns off any cloud canopy just before it sizzles over the canal. However, because the clouds are determined faces right now, today is different.

First raindrops fall on me uncertain. The rainfall can either be as light breathing or become a torrent. Barely felt, the warm raindrops land gently on me today as harmless and even. I pull out the hood from my jacket and tug it over my head, just in case. Raindrops fall a little faster as I move forward but they are polite raindrops. Just before they strike, the drops almost apologize before landing on me, as if each raindrop came equipped with a tiny pair of open arms and silky fingers. Constantly surprised at the lightness of the rain, I ask myself if each raindrop is carefully weighed beforehand. And how are these raindrops warmed just enough on their way down?

Walkers moving by me show their options. An elderly couple suddenly sprouts navy umbrellas. A jogger in his late teens pops the hood on his grey hoodie and keeps up his pace. Two middle-aged women wear transparent raincoats, their hoods covering heaps of gray curly hair and I am amazed at their youthful faces. Pushing their infant son in a stroller, a young couple stops, tilts their heads upwards, welcomes rain into their mouths and their all-teeth smiles are grateful for each and every drop.

On the canal itself, the rain knits a bubbly cover to make sure the water flows all the way to wherever it's going, just as the best blanket can take us all the way through sleep.

I stop to catch several raindrops and I notice how easily each one melts into the creases on my palms. There is a secret language taking shape in my hands…a code of simplicity, of unvarnished love.

I am reminded why I'm here today. Even with the light rain, I find reasons for my joy.

Yesterday, at a bus-stop on the boulevard, the sunshine and graceful winds wrapped me in a brilliant haze only found here. Just waiting for a bus reminds me that perception is a small part of reality. The beauty of waiting. The real beauty waiting.

Back on the canal, I rub my moistened hands together and my palms are cleaner than the rain itself. The rain on my face has a measured pace, a message from the past:

Once upon a time this entire area might have been filled with marshes that were drained to make the place more habitable. And it worked. Roads and buildings were built. People came to the canal bringing their own anecdotes. The waterway developed a life of its own. And to this day, the canal not only listens but also speaks to anyone who is capable suspending his or her disbeliefs.

I quicken my pace and I imagine my jacket becoming heavier but it remains remarkably light. The weightless, soaked jacket massages my back with such a smooth touch that I could walk forever and I think I will. Yes, I will walk my way westward where I will melt into a huge body of water and swim along with any creature that moves. Those living things will accept me totally because dissolving into life is the epitome of everything the canal has given me. After, we will all flow out into some exotic shipping channel to join the passing cargo ships which are either heading to international destinations or unloading in the port of an imaginary city. Personally, I would hope to land back in this canal and start this process all over again.

Cats and the Suitcase

LATE AFTERNOON AND A CHINLESS BUSINESSMAN DRESSED IN A DARK suit, white shirt and cherry-red tie, wheels his luggage down the pathway while checking his smartphone. Looking so alert, the businessman's dark-haired head could be a periscope on two legs.

Suddenly, he stops at a series of cement steps leading down to the water. On the steps are four cats mostly black in colour, each one perched alone, like a fur god on the steps of an altar. The cats wait patiently for the sun to lower itself and disappear into the skyline. He looks down at the cats and then checks his smartphone. Looking bored with the man's constant flicking of his thumbs, the felines pad their way to the bottom step and turn their eyes to the outside wall of the canal. They know that shortly after the sun slides into another world, the rats will emerge from the canal wall and the cats...they will be waiting. Meanwhile, the businessman is still frantically texting or emailing someone on his phone and he has already nudged his suitcase closer to the edge of the wall so people can walk by. All four cats climb the steps and rub their bodies against the man's suitcase, as if inside was a delicacy made only for them. The man sits an am arm's length from his suitcase on the canal wall and lets his feet dangle while his thumbs continue their blazing speed. Circling his luggage, the cats forget him. He ignores the cats too and maybe assumes that the animals are simply curious. Their clockwise circling seems endless and could be a ritual for the evening's catch. And their speed is constant and the man is soon held hypnotic by the black-blurred merry-go-round. He doesn't dare try to move on with his suitcase although he should soon hail a taxicab to get him to the airport on time. But the cats fascinate him. He will keep watching until they stop circling and they do so only briefly. Then they reverse their circling, as if they are performing for a captured audience. The businessman checks his smartphone again and realizes that he has to leave. As he stands and grabs the extended metal handle of his suitcase, the four cats each face him with their backs in the air so he decides to leave his luggage there for the moment. Again his fingers busily access the Internet and he checks for his red-eye flight departing at eleven-thirty p.m.. Meanwhile, the four cats resume their now clockwise circling and the darkness is almost upon them. The more night-time approaches, the slower the cats move until finally they stop and move in unison over to the top step. Their eyes dart back and forth while scanning the bottom step waiting…waiting. Within seconds, a wall of rodents reaches the bottom step and then freezes right there. The cats lunge and have their pick. The businessman, stunned by the frantic crying and squealing, grabs his suitcase and runs over to the boulevard. There he flags down a taxi, opens the back door, and slides into the back seat with his suitcase on his lap.

"I could have put your suitcase in my trunk," the cab driver says looking over his shoulder.

"No, that's okay. Just get me straight to the airport, please," the businessman replies. "Don't want to miss my flight."

"I'll see what I can do. Hang on!"

"Thanks."

"By the way, what's so precious about your luggage?"

"Well, I almost lost it back there."

"Really?" asks the cab driver.

Canal Lightning

I HAVE NOWHERE TO GO.

Initially there are bursts of light followed by long, thin, white lines flashing across the water. Yes, tonight there is passion in the sky. First, two lightning streaks slice a cloud into quarters. A spark follows with a huge molar of lightning chomping on treetops. Next, there is a double stitching of yellow-white on water giving the night sky its own narrative; this sky story is written with flashing words on black and has no ending. With a fading moon and the cracking sky language ripping through clouds, I see the start of a battle, an electric sword fight between two hulking monsters of cloud. Spectators include smaller clouds argue with each other about winners and losers and each makes a point by stabbing the air with tiny flares of their own. Then, a bright question mark in reverse takes over the sky and asks who will win. Close by, two main shafts ignite, separate and create a tall mother figure; beside her, a smaller shape sits dutifully, like an only child and both mother and child seem fascinated by the struggle. After, a lasso of flashing light becomes an enormous hook around a tiny judge who searches for a decision because thin white lines can`t decide if they want to be roots or tree branches when they grow up. Later, six streaks dice up the sky into equal parts; they could be three dance couples on the black of the sky dance floor and not the least bit interested in battles. Finally, the bridge is wrapped quickly in yellow sky ribbons.

I know that I can't hide under a tree or the electricity will find me. When I look up higher at the sky, I imagine the shock of it all. Positive protons are at the top of each cloud and heavier negative electrons are at the bottom, like static electricity but only much bigger. Those electrons move so fast they heat up the air and bring brightness with it.

I think of a lightning strike making my heart stop. For only that moment, feelings will freeze and I will be emotionally empty. However, will I have a loss of memory and maybe some paralysis? Will I survive? A scientist once told me that ninety percent of people do survive lightning strikes.

In the meantime, who's going to win this sky contest?

Suddenly, a tree not far from me is struck and split completely in half from the top down… just when I thought the night had calmed down somewhat. Smoke creeps up to the sky, like a lazy alphabet. Lost somewhere between here and there are the tree remains.

Clouds shaped like telephone poles, form a fence around the warriors of the sky who now look exhausted. Their swords hang loosely from their hands. Beards are dripping sweat the colour of yellow beads. The brutality in their eyes is gone and their mouths droop. Just as the two turn their backs on one another, a huge swollen moon momentarily lights up the sky and my heart starts beating…again.

I wonder if I should trust the moon to stay where it is because the sky can have a will of its own at any moment so I wait. I wait for the clouds to slowly strangle the moon but it doesn't happen. I wait for the moon to fade or hide in a corner of sky. I wait for the night to resume its confusion all over again. No, I think I'll wait for the sunrise from the northeast side of the canal… just to be daylight sure.

I have nowhere to go.

Waiting

"I'VE DONE EVERYTHING POSSIBLE," HE SAYS.

A man, with a nose that has been broken too often, and dressed in a pumpkin-orange T-shirt, cut-off jeans and sandals, stands on the top step of stairs leading down to the canal. He holds a lemon-yellow cardboard sign that reads: "HELP ME PLEASE… MY WIFE IS HOOKED ON PILLS!"

Walkers and joggers take a peek at his sign and move on quickly. I stop, read the sign carefully and then fold my arms, as if the message could apply to me.

"What kind of help are you looking for?" I ask. "And…why don't you just leave your wife?"

"We've been together for nearly forty years. You could say that we grew up together. First sex. First love. She's the mother of our three kids. I remember buying my first car and having my first real job while with her. We rented our first apartment together and then bought our first house."

"Sounds like a lot of history but… why are you here with that sign?"

"My wife has been through lots of treatment centres and has conned many doctors. The cops have been to our house so many times they know us by our first names and hardly take any notes now. The worst was last week when she got kicked out of her seventh treatment centre and decided to take a taxi home; that treatment center is three hundred miles from our house."

"Have you talked to a lawyer?" I ask.

"Yes, I have and she says that no matter what happens, I'll have to give my wife half of my pay so I've been waiting for my wife to kill herself. That's why I didn't leave until a year ago. You know, we slept in different bedrooms and I refused to have sex with her. One of our sons still lives at home and he tells me the place is a mess. I have gone for counselling but my wife refused to go. On my own for a year now, I rent a basement suite."

"Now what?"

"Separation paperwork has been sent but she refuses to sign anything. My lawyer tells me that I have to file for a divorce and then my wife will have no choice. Meanwhile, I have met another woman and she's the most loving person I have ever known," he says.

"But… why you are carrying that sign?" I ask, my face a puzzled squint.

"I want everyone who stops here to ask me if I have done enough to save my marriage."

"Have you?"

"Sure have. Last night I went over to the house to see if she would sign some income tax papers. We yelled and screamed at each other and nothing got signed. This morning, my lawyer served her with the divorce papers."

"Maybe there is only one more thing you can do," I say throwing my hands up at the sun.

"And what is that?"

I grab his big yellow sign and tear it up equally into eight pieces. Then I return four of the pieces to him.

"Do like me," I tell him.

Together, we fling each piece of his cardboard sign across the canal, as if we were skimming flat rocks, like a couple of kids but the yellow cardboard settles on the water, darkens, and sinks to the bottom.

"I've done everything possible," he says.

Currents

A Canadian soldier stands at ease searching for something on the canal's surface.

On the right side of his chin is a single fat tear ready to roll from his face and there is a second tear welling up in his left eye. Perhaps he is saying to the canal that he has had enough of the cliché where old men create wars so younger men can die.

Because of the unusual humidity and heat around the canal today, the soldier appears to be melting under his uniform. Maps of sweat shape themselves into unknown countries from his armpits outward while the collar on his shirt remains stiff and upright. His lips appear to be swollen and on the verge of begging for answers. On the soldier's chin is a sparse beard shaven clean, as if he hasn't been away from puberty for long. Maybe the soldier is too sad to be afraid and, for the moment, his neck is rigid possibly because he may have forgotten how to swallow truths about what he has witnessed.

In his left shirt pocket is a green, plastic pen and what looks like a small notepad sticking out which keeps the pocket flap open. Maybe he has written so many notes to himself, his family and to government officials. The words he uses are the same. The soldier has tried using re-run lines about the uselessness of military conflicts from the TV series MASH but even those are tired and sanctimonious; yet, he can't stop himself from watching MASH re-runs twice a day. How often does he need to be reminded about the limits of humanity? Then the soldier tucks away his notepad and turns to walk towards an empty bench.

Resting on the bench, he again pulls out his notepad because he has more to say. This time he may be writing a note to himself about what he saw happening to a fellow soldier who was also a close friend. The buddy was captured by the enemy and then had his arms and legs strapped to a heavy wooden chair beneath a dead tree in an empty field. Next, a cage-like device was dropped down over his head resting on his shoulders. Then the cage was filled with live sewer rats and the enemy soldiers watched and timed the man screaming his way to a horrid death.

Up on his feet again, the soldier slips his notepad back into his shirt pocket and then places both of his hands on his hips. He still eyes his left wrist remembering how much time it took for his buddy to die but stops and now digs into another pocket to pull out his smartphone which has more to offer than simply the timing of death. One of his thumbs works quickly and he pulls up a photograph of the deceased, the friend saluting the world with a full can of Molson Canadian beer and smiling broadly at the camera. Beside him is a second man from their regiment, the one who collected the remains of the dead soldier. The second man has lost his thirst…somewhere and holds a crushed beer can, as if he knew death was imminent.

Perhaps the soldier by the canal wonders if there is still dried blood on that wooden chair. Has the chair absorbed all that horrible pain, the rats' teeth, the claws? Again he feels the blood in the pores of the skin on his left wrist- that awful clogged, dry sensation where the hair stopped growing in the perfect, circular shape of his wristwatch. Holding his left wrist to his ear, the soldier keeps hearing the endless tick-ticking, the frantic jerking back and forth, the erratic shrieking.

A Canadian soldier stands at ease searching for something on the canal's surface.

Tugging and Knowing

NOT FAR FROM A GARDEN'S RUST-COLOURED FENCE, A MAN'S INNARDS dribble from his eyes, nose and mouth.

He is dressed in weathered black jeans, a grey sweatshirt whose odour could cause the canal to reverse its flow, and white runners with black trim. His tan-coloured felt cowboy hat lies on the grass behind him and his dark streaky hair is long and greasy looking. His eyes are deadened. To keep himself from toppling over, his clenched fists are flat on the grass on either side of him, like ballasts.

Trying to pull the man to his feet is a boy, about aged twelve, wearing a beige baseball cap backwards on his head. Both of the boy's fists cling to his father's sweatshirt. The boy is also dressed in tired black jeans, a faded denim jacket with the navy-blue crest of a sports team on the right shoulder. The sleeves of his jacket are a bright orange and light blue in colour. No matter how hard he tries, the boy's efforts make little difference as he is only able to keep his father sitting up. The kid's purple and white runners are dug in at the heels and he will keep pulling.

"You're not going anywhere," the boy says.

"Just… leave… me… alone," the father slurs.

"I'm not letting go!"

"Nobody gives a shit!" the father shouts at the sky.

"Aw, stop feeling sorry for yourself! Mom says you do that all the time."

But the boy still clings to his father's sweatshirt and each of his heels digs deeper into the dirt. "I just spoke to a police officer a minute ago and he's on his way here right now," says the boy now gasping for air.

"Why the hell did you talk to the cops?"

Soon, one of the city's finest shows up and pats the boy on his shoulder.

"You can let go now, Son. I'll take care of him," the police officer tells the kid.

But the boy persists, his knuckles threatening to burst from his fists.

"I can't," the boy says. "My fingers… they're trapped!"

"Here, let me help you," the police officer says.

And he gently pries the boy's fingers away from the father's sweatshirt. Then the policeman helps the father to his feet and leads him over to a bench. The boy quickly joins them.

"I could call for my partner who's sitting in our cruiser and we could bring you downtown."

"Been there, done that," says the father.

"Your boy here wants you to go home. Pick one…the drunk-tank or home?"

"Do I have another choice?"

"Sure, you could keep drinking and die a painful death or be placed in a hospital psych ward."

"Don't you need a wet brain for the psych ward? My muscles work. My memory isn't too bad. Vision's okay."

"Maybe. Generally, wet brain means your body is very low on nutrition such as vitamin B1. It has two stages. At the second stage, when you can't think or take care of yourself, it's too late."

"I'll know when that happens, Officer."

"How?" the policeman asks as a single leaf falls at their feet, like a lost question.

Craving

WITH A SUDDEN TURN, I BANG MY ARM ON A TREE TRUNK AND THE electric elbow pain begs the story to end.

Two boys arm-wrestling with puberty, stop on the pathway and face one another, as if they are rehearsing for something.

The first boy has black hair that has been half-dyed blonde. Wearing a dark green hoodie and a yellow T-shirt, he refuses to smile behind his placid face. Against his wrinkled khakis, he holds his skateboard at his hip. Around the elbows of his hoodie are two bright orange-striped bands. His board has shiny silver wheels and the entire surface is covered with decals and drawings of monster trucks. Slowly rocking back and forth on his red-laced, brown running shoes, the boy might be quietly inventing a narrative of his own.

Standing an arm's length next to him is his friend who has green hair with streaks of black. He probably lives to tell stories because there is a chain of events building up in his mouth and his face just bursts with fiction.

"Let's make some cash," the taller boy says. This boy wears a blood-red hoodie. He is longer in the torso than his friend by several inches and holds his skateboard at his crotch using all four fingers of his left hand. Drawings of yellow and orange bolts of lightning and other decals cover his board.

"Want to hear a story?" the taller boy asks me. "We think what we do is cool and loaded with surprises."

Although I hadn't planned on it, I oblige and ask the boys to do that before they perform a couple of skateboard tricks.

"Sure, why not," I say. "Let's hear them."

"We charge a dollar a story and we will tell three. That'll be three bucks please," the shorter boy says holding out his open right hand.

"Let me hear them first," I say.

All three stories are about the canal, of course: the first is about how a man died as soon as he hit the water, the second is about a little girl who was choked to death by an enormous canal eel because her face got too close to the water and the third is about a mysterious treasure said to be buried in the middle of the canal.

The boys probably do this mostly for tourists and everything has a price.

"Enjoy the money, boys. By the way, where do your ideas come from and what do you do with all your money?" I ask.

"The canal itself has been telling us stories for a long time. And we spend the money as soon as we get it," the talkative boy replies. We buy stuff like 7-Eleven snacks and decals for our skateboards. Did you know that each of our decals has a spiel behind it? Haven't you ever played someone for a tale?"

"Maybe," I reply.

"We play the tourists because they want our stories."

"Were you playing me?" I ask.

"Just practicing," the talkative boy replies. "Maybe we wanted to play you before you played us."

With a sudden turn, I bang my arm on a tree trunk and the electric elbow pain begs the story to end.

Garage Sale

IS REALITY ONLY AN ESTIMATE?

On the south side of the canal, a fading half-open garage door leads into two lines of tables with items for sale. Next to the table on the left, a rack of faded short-sleeved shirts hang tired in the morning air, their faded colours hiding from the sun. On the left table are CD's, of all sorts such as Tom Petty and The Heartbreakers, Chicago, ZZ Top, Linda Ronstadt, The Rolling Stones, Beethoven, Bach, Dean Martin, Badfinger, The Supremes, Vivaldi and Chopin. Two blue and white teapots and delicate cups to match, watch over each other. On the other table are mostly best-seller paperback books and stacks of old National Geographic and Playboy magazines.

The seller, slumped in a creaky, aluminum lawn chair, is in no hurry to make a sale. A filtered cigarette dangles from the left side of his mouth with the smoke curling a sleepy message above his head. Dressed in white cut-off jean shorts, a canary yellow T-shirt and dark brown leather sandals, the man hasn't shaved for several days but his grey-brown hair is perfectly combed. With a mustache that stretches from one cheek to the other, he forces himself to smile beneath his half-closed eyes.

"How's business?" I ask leafing through a 1979 issue of National Geographic.

"Slow. Moves like me," he replies. "See something that catches your fancy?"

"Not yet. Just browsing."

"Take your time," he says.

I pick up a snow globe containing a tiny older man, maybe in his late seventies, dressed in bleu, blanc, rouge, the colours of the French flag, sitting in an armchair and pointing his cane at the Eiffel Tower. To activate the snow, I shake the globe and marvel at the white flakes. When I place the globe back on the table, the whiteness swirls through the liquid and settles on the ground, carpet-like.

"Nobody really knows what that snow is made of," the man says. "Apparently, it's a trade secret." "It looks like snow so that's all I need to know," I reply. "Snow globes help me plan, help me forget."

"Some say that the liquid in those snow globes is anti-freeze," he says.

"I wonder what that old man in the armchair has to say?"

I pick up the snow globe again and ask, "Alright, how much for this?"

"For you, a special price. Ten bucks."

"That's a bit high. This snow globe looks like it has been around the world a few times. The glass has chips in it and the Eiffel Tower is slightly tilted to the right. Even the old man is ready to slide out of his armchair."

"But didn't you just say that snow globes help you?"

"True. Throw in this 1979 National Geographic about tropical storms and you've got a sale."

"Deal."

Paying the ten bucks, I fold the magazine in two and slip it into the back pocket of my shorts. I hold the snow globe in my right hand, like an offering and cross the boulevard to a recently painted bench. I surrender myself into the globe. Although this is not Paris, I invent the feeling of snow falling on my head and shoulders from a French November sky. It is a light feeling as most snowflakes melt before reaching my skin. The make-believe flakes are surprisingly refreshing and comforting. The sudden cane in my hand points to the top of the Eiffel Tower and a confident smile takes over my face.

Is reality only an estimate?

Balloons

"Just make sure the strings are long enough," he says.

A boy wearing a bright red baseball cap, is perched with his feet dangling over the canal water. In his left hand are the strings of three blue and two yellow balloons. Hanging from his right shoulder is a brown canvas backpack shaped like a hiker's heart. Clinging to the right side of his face is a tear large enough to contain the story of his life. Is this tear impossible to tie to the end of a string as a sixth balloon? Even if I sat on a stool inside the boy's head, I couldn't possibly know what motivates him and his balloons to think, feel or act like he does right now.

Above the boy, the sky is confused and is coloured in swirling yellow, gray and blue with sunlight poking through in several places. Making its own request the sky may want that tear to either plop down into the canal or go back to where it came from…if that were possible. Something has to be done as the tear is swelling its way across the boy's cheek. Can gloom expand like that? Can it be so transparent yet never disappear?

After clearing my throat, I ask the boy if he needs help.

"Oh, no thanks, Mister," he says turning his face towards me.

"That's a huge tear on your face. Are you hurt ?"

"Not sure. I'm celebrating my little brother who died of leukemia five years ago. One balloon a year is how I remember him. Then, I release each balloon, one by one, and the wind takes care of the rest."

"What about that big fat tear on your face?" I ask.

"That's new as of today. It just clings to my face. The wind doesn't help. I don't know what to do. I'm afraid to touch it and I'm out of balloons," he says.

"Try facing the sun directly and stay that way," I offer. "Maybe the heat will help."

"Sure. I'll try that.

"The tear, now the size ofthe bottom of a teacup, gradually evaporates until the boy's face is as dry as sunlight.

"How's that tear?" I ask.

"Gone away," the boy replies opening his canvas bag. "I'm looking for more balloons now."

"Any luck?"

"Nope. Maybe next year I'll bring extras… just in case."

"Good idea," I say.

The sun now covers his face entirely and his eyes are firmly closed. Moments later, he gets to his feet with both eyes wide open. Looking down at the canal, the boy checks his reflection in the water.

"Next time I'll be ready," he says. "Don't want to sound mushy but I never had such a big tear that wouldn't budge. Even though I don't cry for my little brother that often anymore, shouldn't tears just fall?"

"Maybe sometimes gravity is foreign to tears."

"Time for me to get going. I appreciate your help," the boy says.

"Well, you helped me too," I reply.

"How?"

"For years I've been trying to understand the weight of sadness."

"Just make sure the strings are long enough," he says.

Ethics

Are all answers worth waiting for?

At the east end of the canal, there are empty canoes standing by. Meanwhile, the sky is out-blue-ing itself and breathes easily while being filled with puffs of long, thin clouds stretching towards the sun. The canal is so placid and waits for each tree and bush to be reflected on its surface through a gauze-like vision. The water is not a perfect mirror.

Except for me and a homeless man who asks for money, the pathway is almost empty.

"I don't give money but if you're hungry, I'll buy you something to eat," I say.

"Well… I guess so," the homeless man replies.

"Okay, let's go. I'm hungry too."

We move together silently across the boulevard and finally to the avenue which runs west to east. When we stop at a McDonald's, I offer to buy him a Big Mac or McChicken sandwich with fries and a drink.

"I'm a vegetarian!" he says.

"Right. How about some fries and a salad?" I offer.

"Sure. I also wouldn't mind a bottle of water and an ice cream cone for dessert."

I order what the man wants and a McChicken sandwich with a bottle of water for myself.

"Are you waiting for people to change their eating habits?" I ask after swallowing another mouthful of water. "Today, everyone I look at appears to be waiting for something to change."

"What other people eat is none of my business. I have my own rules for not eating meat. I am waiting for my body to heal itself from all the creatures I have eaten for over fifty years. It's all about principles and healing for me."

"To each his own," I reply as arguing about virtues would be like trying to measure sunlight in my hands.

After we finish eating, I stand and get ready to leave.

"I'm walking back to the canal," I say.

"Want some company?" the homeless man asks.

Back at the canal, the homeless man says: "Actually, I wouldn't mind having a life like yours without the meat but… where do I start? I didn't ask to be homeless. I didn't even ask to be born but neither did you. I left home at sixteen because of my parents' hopeless states of mind and body. Insane. School didn't work. I've has so, so many different jobs that work became a blur, a passing thought. I have never found out what I'm really good at. But I've learned how to survive quite well on the streets so I suppose I'm good at that."

Will the homeless man's standards make a difference?

Are all answers worth waiting for?

Skies and Trains

EVEN THE DAY HAS A MIND OF ITS OWN.

When the canal forks, I stand where the second part heads north and watch the rising sun rinse colour on the water. The sky, with blotches of yellow, orange and grey-blue, gradually peels away the night. A lone tree stabs the orange and makes a cloud bleed yellow. Another tree wears the morning gold like a shawl. As the water turns orange, its ripples quickly lose the colour of night.

A man with hurricane-grey hair pulls a large, steel-framed basket on two wheels behind him. He must be over six feet tall and wears brand new blue jeans, a white T-Shirt and white, cross-trainer running shoes. His hair is so thick it could be used as a wire brush to clean the walls of the canal. His voice has that smoker's rasp. In his basket are two small, partially-filled water bottles. Also in the basket are a black cotton jacket, a Toronto Blue Jays baseball cap, a newspaper and a TIME Magazine with a photograph of an old freight train on the cover.

"Good morning," he says stopping right next to me and pointing at the sky. "What do you think of the start of this summer day?"

"Gorgeous," I say. "A real beauty!"

"You know, the only time I needed help to start my day was when I found out I was adopted by my fireman father. Turns out, my mother was against the adoption but my father convinced her, or should I say, "bullied her" into agreeing with him. For years they kept my adoption a secret."

Who is this guy, whom I just met, and why is he suddenly revealing all this information? Again, why does this happen to me so often and I always accept it? He must be reading me because he leans closer, as if he's ready to spill his entire life story on me, like a sudden rainfall and I simply let go of my hesitation because it is what it is.

"My name's Peter," he says extending his hand to me.

"I'm Ken," I say shaking his hand.

"Well Ken, unlike what we're both seeing with the clarity of the canal today, I needed lots of help to get started each day for a long time after I found out about my adoption. I began building model train sets in our basement to keep me focused on the day. I had so much detail built into my model trains that I believed one of them would lead me to my birth mother. So I kept building and building until most of the basement was filled with my model trains. My adoptive parents didn't know what to think but they left me alone."

"And maybe that's what we're doing right now…leaving the day alone," I say.

"None of my trains ever led to my birth mother."

"Did you ever locate her later on?" I ask.

"Yes, I did find her when I was older. I found out where she lived and she worked as a waitress in a diner in San Francisco. When I finally contacted her, she made excuses for my existence so we didn't meet. Good thing I could fall back on my model trains… even if the trains took me nowhere."

"My own mother once told me that nothing happens by accident," I say.

"I… was an accident," replies Peter looking me squarely in the eye. "Nothing but. Do you know what an accident is? Do you?"

Even the day has a mind of its own.

Author

"I CERTAINLY DO," SAYS THE YOUNGEST POLICEMAN.

Three hatless policemen walk eastward where the water level is as low as the mud. The rookie officer on the far right carries a notepad and listens, like a student, to the one in the middle.

"We got a 911 call from the library." he says. "A middle-aged man went crazy!"

Each move the middle policeman makes seems choreographed. The man on the far left of the three has one hand dangling in front of him away from his holstered weapon, as if he had recently emptied the gun on a threatening fugitive. With slightly slumped shoulders, the police officers trudge forward paying little attention to the canal or people passing by. The two older officers have shaved heads and the skin of each head is whiter than a bed sheet. The younger officer with the notepad has a longish hair-cut but each brown hair on his head knows its place. Oddly enough, only the toes of the younger policemen's boots are shiny while the other men have dust-covered boots, as if dust were a sign of experience.

At the library, one police officer waits on the inside near the door while the other two approach the Head Librarian. Someone in his mid-fifties went stark mad because he couldn't find the book he was looking for. After ripping and flinging books off the shelves, two men in their twenties finally subdued him and held him down on the floor.

The man being held is of medium height but has weight-lifter arms. The two men holding him down are both actually sitting on him but his muscled arms keep pushing back. Turning the man over on his belly, the middle policeman orders him to calm down and slaps on the handcuffs.

"On your feet, Sir!" he then commands. "You did all this damage simply because you couldn't find the book you wanted?"

"It isn't just any book. It's my… most… recent book. I'm an author from another city."

"So why would an author cause such a big fuss simply because his latest book isn't in the library?"

"Don't you know who I am?" the author shouts.

"No… we don't," the second officer replies. "And again, calm down, please."

"Doesn't matter who you are," the third officer says as he faces the author directly. "You caused a lot of damage and we're taking you downtown to police headquarters."

"But really, don't you know me at all?" the author asks again.

"Do you wish to press charges?" the first officer asks the Head Librarian ignoring the author.

"Most certainly," replies the Head Librarian. "Look at the mess! And over there… two of our computers were tossed on the floor."

"Okay, we need you to also come downtown and fill out a report," the first officer says.

"Of course," replies the Head Librarian.

Then, looking at the author, the first officer says, "Do you have anything to offer?"

"What the hell is the matter with you people?" he shouts "You need me! Doesn't anyone know who or what I am?"

"I certainly do," says the youngest policeman.

The Man and the Eel (for B.)

"BUT...CAN YOU FEEL MY FEELINGS LIKE MY SON? CAN YOU?"

A man with hair the colour of freshly cut hay rests on a bench facing the canal with his head held low in both his hands. Because a racket lies on the bench to his left, he could be a tennis player. On his right is a sports bag probably containing cans of tennis balls, a towel and his tennis shoes. The man looks downward at the cement below his feet and this makes him appear to be sad. However, upon looking closer, he could be contemplating the life that has crawled by him. Maybe he has a thirty-year old handicapped son who has far more issues than his autistic diagnosis such as lags in both cognitive and emotional development. What will both he and his wife do? The man doesn't seem upset about his boy and he may be the kind of person who says: "You take the cards you've been dealt." In fact, when he lifts his head to peer across the canal, his face says that he may also be that person who might ask himself if he can add value to any relationship.

Not far from the man, two short, slender fish spring out of the canal and then up into the air, as if the water was questioning their presence. A long, thick black eel weaves its way to the the canal wall causing all living forms to shudder. Creating a shadowy language, the eel curves and slices quietly through the water. Everything about this creature is dark and even the sun's rays jump out of its way. Creatures that look like inanimate objects suddenly spring to life, show their legs or fins and zip out of the eel's path. Then the eel turns itself into a huge underwater smirk, as if it is amused by all the commotion it is causing.

What is the eel doing to the man's mind whose hands leave his face as he peers into the canal? "Are you laughing at me?" the man seems to be asking the eel.

Almost immediately, the eel turns upside down, as if mocking the man and his pensive concerns about his disabled son.

"You… may not know this, but I've long ago accepted my boy and his limitations," says the man now on his feet and standing on the lip of the canal.

As if the eel understands, its body straightens out and remains motionless.

"Tell me, eel, what were your ulterior motives for behaving like you did? Were you being dishonest, self-seeking or were you filled with some form of self-pity? It has to be one of those three." The eel slips back into its smirk, then its frown and finally that straight line again.

"Must be some kind of self-seeking," the man says. You certainly don't have to be dishonest and I can't see why you'd have any self-pity. Are you bored with your easy life in the canal… especially with the way all other fish are afraid of you and you get what you want when you want it?"

The eel then thrashes back and forth in the water, as if feeling uncomfortable with the man's question.

"Ha. Looks like I struck a nerve," the man says. "You were looking for attention after all. Because my son is wired differently, he does that too. Intellectually or emotionally, he's undeveloped but yet he feels everything in others. He thinks only about himself most times, like a child."

The eel stands on its tail and stares straight up at the man. Then it lowers itself and curls into a fist.

"My son does that too when he doesn't get his way or if I'm not behaving the way he thinks I should be behaving. But… can you feel my feelings, like my son? Can you?"

Stairs (for Joe Harley)

THE CEMENT STAIRS LEADING DOWN TO THE DARKNESS OF THE CANAL become more orange the further down the man with the silver hair looks. The orange must not be blood because blood turns a deeper red when exposed to the air, all due to the hemoglobin. No murders or suicides here. Maybe, the stairs were once painted orange to celebrate an artist's accomplishments. Once upon a time, there may have been an explosion of cheer, optimism and flamboyance on these stairs. Perhaps the silver-haired man stood here before on the top step, contemplating his descent with his feet shuffling back and forth, like his thoughts, and that is why the top step has little colour left, especially in the certain sunlight. He remains where he is, wooden cane in hand, because at the bottom of the stairs there may be more than just canal water.

Maybe the man remembers as a boy looking under his bed at night making sure there was nothing there. Did he once slide under his bed to join the unknowns because his tough-as-nails mother, told him to face his fears after she caught him checking under his bed? Today there is no bed but the silver-haired man wishes there was one.

At the bottom there are hollow unknowns, unresolved questions. Every imaginable under-the-bed creature awaits his descent. If these stairs could talk, might they be self-indulgent, superficial, overbearing, insincere or overly proud? Who knows? The language of the stairs is ambiguous at best.

Walls surrounding the stairs have occasional scars on the top and bottom, as if parts of the man's skin were originally used to paper the wall. Yes, he has his scars, like all of us. Perhaps the man with the silver hair had sections of his skin torn off by those demanding perfection from him. Maybe the man wears his heart not only on his sleeve but wherever his skin is exposed to the harsh light of expectations.

When the man with the silver hair takes his first step down to the canal, he limps slightly and swings his cane back and forth in front of him. He may be cautioning himself that he is moving downward through a giant, black keyhole. Then courage takes him right down the stairs. Once he's past the keyhole, the silver-haired man slips into the canal and his uneven gait disappears in the water. There he lies on his back with his wet silver hair forming glowing quotation marks around his head which is now a photographer's aura. Soon he floats westward towards a larger body of water, his eyes constantly flicking, as if taking photos of an optimistic sky. Just before he reaches the open water, he swims to shore and climbs easily onto dry land, his limp now totally gone. With his shoulders back and his head tall, he walks straight ahead and exaggerates the lifting of each of his legs, like a goosestep, as if he's ready for any stairs. The silver-haired man does not look behind or under beds, benches, bushes, trees or rocks. Perhaps his imagination has been restored to a world removed from beds and stairs.

When he goes to bed tonight, the silvery-haired man might think of flinging his extra cane and every shoe he owns under his bed to celebrate the disappearance of his limp and for any other reason that brings simplicity to his mind.

Pumpkin Face

AND ALL OF THIS IS DUE TO THE CONSTANT APPEARANCE OF ORANGE and black.

Both the park bench and garbage can seem lonely and stark this morning.

Asleep on the bench, the homeless man with his face to the water, has a huge, orange, plastic Halloween pumpkin with a black plastic handle sitting on the ground next to him. Because he has the same smile as his pumpkin, his sleep must be pleasant. Inside the pumpkin are several Halloween treats even though this is weeks after Halloween. Also, inside is some leftover food partially-covered in McDonald's wrappers.

The cement block at the base of the bench and garbage can might be the man's headstone on his living grave of a bench. Instead of a date of birth and deceased date, a plastic Halloween pumpkin is all he has to identify himself. He has never been born and will never die and may only awaken on October 31. Calendar dates may do that to anyone living on a park bench.

Like a tiny fast-food cloud, the smell of the McDonald's food fills the air. Pigeons move towards the plastic face. Inching closer and closer the birds are joined by more and more of their kind. The man suddenly awakes from his pumpkin siesta and the birds skirt away from his plastic stash of food.

"Stay away from my grub," he says. "But you can have a couple of my Halloween candies. Let me unwrap them for you so you don't choke on the wrappers."

He flings the orange and black wrappers into the garbage can and then rolls the two candies onto the pathway. Well, the pigeons move quickly towards the two candies and they find it hard to dig their heads into the sweets. In fact, each candy becomes stuck to the beak of a bird. Other pigeons try to peck at the candies but the two birds shake their heads frantically and escape into the air with Halloween candy still glued to their beaks. Meanwhile, the homeless man motions for the two pigeons to come back so he can unglue the candy from their faces. However, in the sky, the two pigeons bump in mid-air and the candies come loose falling back onto the pathway. Two other pigeons plunge their beaks into the candy and they too take off frantically shaking their heads to rid themselves of the sticky morass. But these two birds disappear across the canal hopefully finding their own solutions. The homeless man hesitates to provide more candy for the pigeons and instead pulls out a partially-eaten burger and tears it up into small bites for the birds.

"Even though Halloween happened many months ago, Happy Halloween, you birds!"

The pigeons frantically pick away at the burger bits until even the crumbs have vanished.

"I have to keep the other leftover burger for my lunch," he reminds the pigeons. "And no more Halloween candy for you!" the man says sliding his plastic pumpkin under the bench.

The birds fly away and the man stands to stretch in the early morning blinding sun. His eyes scan the opposite side of the canal and then he shrugs his shoulders holding both of his palms up the sky.

Later, he curls up on the bench and holds his plastic pumpkin to his chest, like a teddy bear. Falling asleep quickly, the man has his left arm protecting the top of his pumpkin. His face soon becomes the plastic pumpkin again and the sunlight accepts and cradles both faces.

Maybe when he awakes, the man will turn his back to the sun and wait patiently for the sounds of Halloween wings returning for another challenge. Or the birds will already be there twitching back and forth on their tiny claws waiting…waiting.

A Cushion and A Heart

"I'M SO SURPRISED THAT YOU'RE EVEN HERE," THE HOMELESS MAN SAYS.

With more hair than a field of wheat and dressed from head-to-toe in various shades of grey, the homeless man stands near a canal bench and gestures at the immovable garbage can being held by a metal frame on a cement platform beside him. Perhaps he prefers green garbage bags because they come and go but the garbage can is permanent.

"I want this container moved away from MY bench, in case it lowers the value of MY property," he says to no one in particular, his hands and arms flailing in the morning sunlight. "Nobody but nobody deserves to live under such horrible conditions and I will soon write to the mayor expressing my indignation. I'm sure our illustrious mayor doesn't sleep next to a garbage can. If he did, he certainly wouldn't be mayor."

Beside the homeless man is an empty and open green garbage bag. Kneeling on one knee, he continues talking to the bag, as if it were the only ear available. He whispers then speaks aloud and the green plastic exhales then sags, as if the bag was unsure about the homeless man's rant. Still on one knee, the man quietly moves his lips and the plastic bag opens wide. When done, he stands, picks up the garbage bag, looks up at the sky and taps his chest in a slow rhythm. "Yes, I will write a letter to the mayor! Now!"

Before doing that, the man is back on his knees on his tattered beach mat next to the bench. In front of him, he pulls out two white T-shirts from his ragged, brown and green backpack and proceeds to flip one T-shirt open to the light wind. Then he carefully folds the right shoulder over the left shoulder and then the entire T-shirt in half followed by quarters. Each fold is perfect and he lays the T-shirt on his beach mat. Then he follows the same process with his second T-shirt and gently places it on top of the first one. Perhaps he tries to bring order to his homeless life using repetition because he takes both T-shirts, shakes them in the sunlight and repeats his process until the T-shirts are tucked carefully into his backpack. Could these fastidious moves be his final preparation for letter writing?

Later the man turns his attention back to both the garbage can and bag. In his left hand he holds a small pad of paper.

"I suppose I can get more out of the mayor with honey than with vinegar so I better word my letter carefully," he says aloud with a rehearsed, even tone.

While writing, his wrist sits on the balled-up green garbage bag which brings him great comfort. Little beads of sweat form between his hand and the green plastic bag, his writing hand now beating like a heart.

As he looks out over the canal, the mayor suddenly appears beside him on the bench. Both men say nothing. When the homeless man completes his letter, the mayor replies by writing his own message back to the homeless man but not before he asks to borrow the green garbage bag to place under his own writing hand.

All afternoon, the mayor and the homeless man write back and forth to each other, using the balled-up, green garbage bag as a reminder that words may require both a cushion and a heart.

"This is amazing," the mayor says. "Look at how we've connected."

"I'm so surprised that you're even here," the homeless man says.

Secrets

LIKE A HUMAN BODY, THE CANAL NEEDS TIME TO RECOVER.

Yesterday, the rain fell so hard and for so long that it seeped through many roofs, like water through cardboard. The canal has become a person in therapy, the water so muddied and its level so high that it overflowed slightly onto the pathway and then puddled on the boulevard.

Still feeling slimy, the canal may be wondering why its secrets have been dredged up. In fact, the current barely moves. It could be exhausted and is recovering under the early morning light. Tree branches, bottles, cans and other debris are everywhere in and on the water. Perhaps the silt will sink only after acceptance has reached a new level of understanding on this waterway and then the current will flow freely towards an unknown ocean. Although a lot has been uncovered, the muck still coats much of the canal's walls.

Under a young tree next to the pathway, a homeless man is asleep inside his sleeping bag. He may have spent the night dodging the rain and sought shelter wherever he could. His clothes cover a nearby bench, drying in the gradual morning heat. His other belongings are packed loosely in a shopping cart parked next to his motionless head and his sleep is so sound that no one could possibly know his secrets.

Perhaps both this channel and the sleeping man want to maintain their seclusion… one that is cheerless with debris and the other without words. The homeless man has probably been through so many therapies that he has two types of answers for every question: one that the therapist wants to hear and the other is his truth. And he may have more places to hide other than around the canal.

The sun's gold seeps into the sky and then pushes through a solitary cloud. Even with all its power though, sunrays seem confused by the dirt-filled water. All the heat in the world will not bring back clarity to the water. Maybe, the sun is unaccustomed to what it sees right now or, like a vigilant mother or father, worries about this inland waterway being in turmoil.

The homeless man awakens to the sounds of work crews cleaning up debris around the canal pathway. Rubbing his eyes he sits upright pushing open his sleeping bag. Then the man slips out of the bag in his blue T-shirt and jean shorts. On his feet, he stretches his arms and shoulders at the sky and then checks to see if his clothes have dried. Men and women in the work crew mostly ignore the homeless man, as if he were just another itinerant face.

However, one woman worker is curious and drops several broken tree branches at her feet.

"Is your stuff dry yet?" she asks.

"Getting there," the man replies. "Good thing I was able to take cover last night under that bridge up ahead. Otherwise, my sleeping bag would have been drenched. I've never seen so much rain in one night!"

"I'm so glad you found some cover. And look at the canal, it still looks like an enormous tub of watery mud," she said.

"And the entire waterway has been turned inside-out," the worker says.

"How long do you think it will take for all that dirt to settle?"

"Maybe a day or two," the woman replies. "Reminds me of when one of us gets violated at night."

Like a human body, the canal need time to recover.

THREE

Changes

"YES, YES. IT'S ALL COMING BACK TO ME NOW."

Almost huddled on the canal bench is a woman who could be in her eighth decade with her silver hair piled high in different-sized curls. Next to her left elbow on the grass stands her walker. She tells everyone who goes by that she has been crying for a long time but there are no tears in her eyes. Wrinkles on her face are tiny threads of silk.

A man, maybe twenty-five years younger, strolling by stops and asks, "Are you all right?"

"It's my tear ducts. They've been blocked for years," she says. Doctors have tried all kinds of medications and procedures. I keep crying but my tears stay inside."

The man wipes his recently shaved head with his sleeve and then plops himself on the bench beside her. "I don't know what's going on in you but I used to cry inside a lot too. I started losing my hair at eighteen. I combed it over. I combed it forward. Grew it long. I tried transplants but it looked like somebody planted a row of crops on my forehead. I wore so many hats. Not long ago, I got rid of the hats and decided to shave my head. Lots of balding men do it. Now, when I cry, my face nearly drowns in tears. What a relief! I've even learned to joke about it. The other day, a guy at work placed his hand on my head and said, 'you know… that feels just like my wife's crystal ball. So, I removed his hand and placed my own hand on my head and said: 'You're right. I know your wife's crystal ball…I've been in it."

But the woman explodes with laughter anyway and her tiny thread piles vibrate across her face.

"Yes, I have heard something like that one before, only riskier."

"Good," the man replies. "Something has to loosen up inside you."

"But I have tried laughter. My family has made efforts. They tell jokes. They laugh a lot. They make funny faces. I see the tears streaming down their faces. I even watch really old comedy films like those old Marx Brothers movies. I wish I could just cry like everyone else whether it's because of sadness or happiness or whatever. Anything."

"Alright, but do you want to try something different," the man asks, a wide smile spreading across his face, like melting chocolate.

"Anything," the woman answers.

"Okay, grab your walker. Let's go. Just stand behind me and watch," the man says.

Over and over the man stops passersby and asks each one to rub the top of his head. Several people refuse. A few look at him and run away. Some do rub his shiny head.

"What do you feel?" he asks each person who takes him up on his offer. "And what do you see?"

Because several don't speak English, some people don't understand his request. Many just laugh. Some cringe and walk away. Others look puzzled and tap their own heads.

Finally, a woman probably in her late forties, wearing an orange track suit and roller blades, stops and rubs the man's forehead back and forth. She does this non-stop for several seconds.

"I know what this feels like!" the woman in the track suit shouts. "I have my own… at home!"

That does it! The older woman explodes with laughter and the tears pour down her face. Wrinkles are washed away. She gets to her feet. Slides her walker over to the bald man and takes over the head rubbing.

"Yes… yes, it's all coming back to me now," she says.

Being Normal Is Over-Rated

Many years ago, a wise person would usually place a human skull, usually made of plastic, on his or her bench or counter because death was approaching.

"The skull reminds us all that sooner or later, death will surely come, and to do good before it's too late," the man says to the skull sitting beside him on the bench. "So here I am with you."

This morning, a man in his seventies with a perfect triangle of a charcoal-coloured beard on his chin, pats the skull beside him. Wearing a red and white polka dotted bandana around his own head, a cherry-red T-shirt, charcoal-coloured shorts and sandals that are so old, they could have been worn by some biblical character, the man seems to be the essence of unflappable determination.

"Today, this is where I work," he announces to the canal.

A man and woman approach the man's bench holding hands with their Down syndrome, teenage son. The boy's wide, flat tongue crawls in and out from the left side of his mouth. His grin expands his cheeks after his father says what could be: "Don't worry, Son. Being normal is over-rated."

"Good morning," the man with the plastic skull says to the family.

The couple stop and bow their heads slightly and the boy tries his best to do the same. They speak little English but that doesn't matter to the man with the skull. Almost immediately, the boy moves towards the skull and gently slides a finger into one of the eye sockets and then quickly withdraws it. Then he slips his right thumb into the opening for the nose and leaves it there for a few seconds while rubbing his own nose with his free hand. After, he moves three fingers into the skull's mouth and grunts with words that sound like they are asking if the plastic skull is hungry.

"I have this skull beside me so I can do some good," he says offering the head to the boy. "Here, want to hold it in your hands and see what happens?"

At first the boy is hesitant but then he cracks his own face in half with a huge grin and takes the skull into his hands. Within seconds, the boy's laughter becomes more like syrup, as if he could care less about his disability. Gradually, the joy is replaced by guttural chuckling. The boy's parents also join in the laughter and the father pats his boy on the back, as if he were congratulating his son for being so human.

"So, what's so funny?" the man with the skull asks. "Why the laughter?" he adds showing a toothy smile and then pointing to his own face.

But the father simply shakes the man's hand and then gently lifts the skull from his son's grasp.

After returning the skull to the man on the bench, the man nods at his wife and son. Then the entire family stands back side by side and graciously bows their heads in unison, as if any other display might be intrusive.

"Thank… you!" the father manages to utter. "Don't want to disturb."

"You're welcome!" replies the man on the bench. "Wish I knew what you were thanking me for."

All three family members approach the bench and, one after the other, kisses the top of the skull, as if they are remembering the dead still lingering in their hearts. After they each bend their heads again, the family walks away from the bench giggling politely but moving with a new understanding that looks as smooth as the ripples on today's canal.

Many years ago, a wise person would place a human skull on his or her work table because death was approaching.

Are You a Cliché?

"DON'T SLOW DOWN?" SHE REPLIES. "WE'RE ONLY HALF-WAY DONE."

On the canal pathway, a tall middle-aged jogger with a thicket of white hair slows down his running with the woman beside him. She too is tall, athletic-looking and her blonde hair is tied on top of her head, like a bouquet.

"I have to do something about the deceased date on my mother's tombstone. She died more than fifteen years ago and for some reason I forgot to have the deceased date engraved on her tombstone." "Why are you thinking of this now?" the woman asks while slowing down.

"As we were running, I was looking at the canal and its tiny creases reminded me of those slow-moving pages of a calendar I saw in a couple of old movies made in the 1940's," replies the man. "You know- calendars…time… made me think of my mother's tombstone."

"Why don't you just go to the cemetery and have it done by the engraver?" the woman inquires coming to a complete stop.

Both runners face each other and it looks as if he has lots more to say but doesn't know where to start.

"I keep putting it off. After all, my mother is dead so who's going to care?"

"You," the woman says. "Maybe you still want to honour your mother?"

"What do I do with her memory?" he asks.

"What do you remember?"

"I was the only one to see her taking her final breaths. When my brother and sister arrived after me, they sobbed at her bedside but I didn't shed a tear."

"How come?"

"I felt nothing. I didn't love her but I didn't resent her either. I just felt numb. When I saw the tears on my brother's and sister's faces, I decided to play along and faked my crying. With my head partially turned away, I wiped away imaginary tears. Later, a wise, older friend of mine said it was okay as long as I didn't resent her."

"Strange. I wonder what Freud would say about that?" the woman gently asks.

"I think Freud was more concerned about the unconscious mind and personality. There's nothing unconscious about the relationship I had with my mother because I had no real link to her. She forgot about me the day she brought my little brother home from the hospital. I was about four at the time."

"But aren't middle children often forgotten in most families?"

"I suppose so."

"Then what you are feeling is probably commonplace. You're not a cliché…are you?" the woman asks, her face cringing.

"Normally, I'd be insulted by your words but perhaps my family is more common than I thought," the man replies shrugging his shoulders.

"And your mother?"

"Yeah, she's the one who was the cliché. That's why I couldn't cry when she died. How do I forgive a cliché?" the man asks.

"Cross a bridge…you only realize you've forgiven someone after… you've crossed that bridge."

"Let's keep running," he says.

"Don't slow down!" she replies. "We're only half-way done."

Corner

"I'VE LOST MY FACE," THE WOMAN SAYS. "AND I NEED TO FEEL BETTER."

On the north side of the canal is a boathouse where different groups take out boats which are really canoe kayaks. People often paddle in teams. Sometimes the teams race one another. Other times one or two boats simply slice through the water in a leisurely manner, as if looking for a way to slow down time.

A short, green-eyed woman in her mid-thirties with her black-as-night hair tied back on the left side of her head, leans against the boat house. Her face, an unsolved crossword puzzle, seems like it's ready to explode. She crosses and re-crosses one leg over the other, as if they are lost parts of her body.

Then a trim man, in his early forties who could also be a fitness instructor, unlocks the gates and opens up everything to the day.

"Are you waiting for your team or partner?" he asks the woman.

"No, I'm here alone. Could I rent one of those boats and go out on the canal by myself?" she asks. "We don't rent to people on the spot. Teams and individuals call this number and book their canoes that way. I don't handle any financial transactions."

"Oh, too bad but I really need to get out on the water by myself this morning."

"Is there a problem?" asks the man.

"Oh, what the hell! A couple of days ago, I was stopped by the police for drinking and driving. They took me downtown, booked me and placed me in this room not much bigger than two closets. There were two chairs in the room and a small table.

I didn't sit in either of the chairs and instead went straight to a corner and just stood there. I felt terrible. And to top it all off, my brother is a crown prosecutor for the city."

"But why do you need to be out on the canal this morning?"

"In my head, I was still standing in the corner at the police station, like I was punishing myself. One of my friends suggested I go for a paddle on the canal. You know… get out into the open… forget what happened."

"You do know that the canal does not have the cleanest water. You wouldn't want to tip over in that water- especially after a flood."

"Looks and smells good enough for me," the woman replies.

"Don't let that fool you. Many years ago, a homeless man fell in and died from septic shock…all from higher levels of bacteria after a flood."

Then there's a long moment of unspeaking. The air smells amazingly clean. There hasn't been a flood here for many years. Business is slower than a hot summer workday. Life becomes so hushed that tiny creases on the canal look as if they are carving questions on the surface of the water… questions with more than one answer. Except for joggers, people move with ease. Hurrying must be a crime.

The woman inhales slowly, deeply and exhales the same way, as if contemplation were her spare layer of skin. The boathouse manager squirms slightly and clears his throat.

"Sorry I can't help but call that number if you still want to rent."

"I've lost my face," the woman says. "And I need to feel better."

From The Walls of the Garden Sky (for Miranda)

"You never know," the grandfather says. "You never know."

The granddaughter, who might be six or seven years of age, and her grandfather sit together in an act of love on a wooden bench in his tiny garden.

"I will tell everyone where they should be and what they should be doing," the little girl exclaims. "It will be like playing school, Grandpa. I will be the teacher and everyone else will be my students."

The garden has flowers growing from dark topsoil and green plastic pots that hang everywhere. The soil below appears to be barren except for a few scattered, unused flower pots.

"I love your garden," the little girl says. "Looks like the flowers grew from the walls of the sky. Maybe, the plants could be my students and I will show them how to grow."

The grandfather smiles at the perfect afternoon while the sky responds when a long cloud, looking like a slow-moving parade float, drifts across his line of vision.

"Forcing anyone or anything to grow is not easy but you may be the first one to accomplish that," the grandfather says caressing and then kissing the top of the young girl's head. "Nothing you do will surprise me."

"You know, I've seen you talking to plants, Grandpa. I should speak to them too."

"Go ahead," the grandfather replies. "But don't shout."

"Why?"

"Ears don't work well with shouting."

The granddaughter stands in front of their bench and sighs deeply. Then she rubs her hands together and moves slowly to the furthest wall of hanging plants, the wall facing the canal. Her lips move ever so slightly, as if she were rehearsing her wisdom for the world. Then she drops her head and turns it slightly to the left. Perhaps she thinks her whispering can only be heard by the plants and her. The girl's words, at first, are tender breaths but leaves become ears that aren't quite listening. The granddaughter knows it. She raises her voice. Pointing to one plant, she says, "Your leaves should be growing that way- straight up to the sun, maybe to the moon. And you're looking a little crooked."

Gesturing towards a second plant, the little girl says: "And you…you have to grow towards the canal to catch the morning light." The granddaughter moves from plant to plant giving instructions to each one until she is back on the bench with her grandpa.

"How did it go with the plants?" the grandfather asks. "I heard a bit of your whispering, your 'take charge' words."

"When they're ready, they'll do exactly what I asked. They have to be ready though," she says.

"Were they?" Grandpa asks.

"Actually, I only had to repeat myself once. You should have seen those leaves listening."

"How do you know?"

"When I whispered 'thank-you' to each plant, the veins on the leaves turned up, like tiny fingers."

"Sounds good to me," Grandpa answers. "They know you're in charge."

"Yes, but we'll have to come back tomorrow," the granddaughter says straightening out her tiny shoulders. "To make sure," as if there is nothing further from the truth than sentiment.

"You never know," the grandfather says. "You never know."

Branches

"YOU MUST BE HUNGRY," SHE SAYS.

Right where the path turns north from the canal, there is a small, make-shift house cupped in the arms of a tree. The roof is a huge beach umbrella made of blue, green, red and orange triangles. Beneath the rainbow roof are four canvas walls. A sheet of gray canvas makes up the first wall. A second wall is all green material from a leftover tent. Bark-brown canvas creates a third wall. The front of the tree house is white canvas with a flap for the front entrance. Several short two-by-four pieces of wood, tied together with rope, make up the front porch.

On a lower branch, a young woman scrubs her wet laundry with a white soap bar, dunks everything into a large white plastic bucket almost filled with water and then rinses it all out into the canal below. The young woman has dark, shiny eyes the colour of coffee and her long black hair is swept back over her shoulders as an afterthought. She is dressed in a white linen top and white linen pants which are streaked with dirt. Her face invented happiness and her clearly-defined features may be a by-product of this contentment. The woman's fingers are long and noticeably slender and could easily belong on any keyboard.

Meanwhile, her partner, dressed in ragged jean shorts and a soiled, white T-shirt, cleans fish for their breakfast and dumps all the innards into the canal. His knife gleams in rays of sun and his cutting is quick and confident. What will they use to cook the fish or will they eat them raw? The partner is slow, methodical and he too has noticeably long, slender fingers and dark features, although his hair falls only to the bottom of his neck. Do their elegant hands keep them together?

The couple say very little to each other. Before he starts working on another fish, the man looks at his partner, as if she were the only canal goddess here today. And she, in turn, returns his gaze with her own electricity. The energy between them could make the canal boil.

Their tree-fort, love-making might be magical or too predictable. Imagine the alphabet of their passion, the sign language in their fingertips. Trees might breathe easily in the night-time air but then hold their breaths just as the couple explode all over each other.

Down from the tree house is a large, three-wheeled bike complete with a white licence plate. The tricycle is parked at the entranceway, like a family vehicle, behind a clump of branches. The licence plate almost glares at the world from behind the leaves. Just below the bike's handlebars droops a half-rusted, steel basket. The white fenders on the bike are cleaner than the clothes they wear.

A middle-aged African American man passing by, stops, notices the tree house and asks if I know how they were able to squeeze in all those building materials and what do they do in the cold weather?

"Those thick branches would be a challenge," I reply. "And the cold leaves me clueless."

Should the police be notified and have another homeless shelter destroyed? Should the authorities wait until the couple are out for the day and then remove everything? No, that's been done before with little success because homeless people simply set up house somewhere else. Perhaps the police should wait until the residents are "home" so the couple has time to remove their belongings. Instead, the man passing by simply pushes aside several branches, moves cautiously closer and asks if anyone is home. The young woman sticks her head out from the front flap.

"I really do envy your lifestyle," he declares. "The ease of it all.

"You must be hungry," she says.

Mysteries

Behind a curtain of ferns and vines, a woman speaks to someone sounding like a boy wearing the skin of a man. I see his man-sized shadow but his voice sounds out of place.

All that is heard is a motherly tone and then a voice that mostly sounds like a boy and then like a man. The woman's voice is as soft as a peach and the boy's voice could be a small, stringed musical instrument or the thump of a stand-up bass.

"When will this garden be ready?" she could be asking him in what might be Mandarin Chinese.

The boy-man answers with small, deliberate syllables, like drip-drops from a leaky bathroom faucet while the mother waits patiently for her boy's conclusion. Continuing on, the boy doesn't stop and not once does the mother interrupt. The child's high-low voice behind the curtain measures the slow afternoon pace and the mother's waiting is guarded by the music of her own breathing.

Just when she thinks the boy has stopped, I hear the woman inhaling deeply, as if she were preparing to speak. But she is interrupted by the continuing singsong sounds of her boy-man whose voice moves up and down its own scales. Finally, the woman makes a "shush" sound and that silences the boy. For endless seconds there is nothing but the sounds of hesitant winds blowing across the canal. Perhaps the mother and her son are listening, just as I am, to what the winds have to say about gardens.

It takes all I have not to interrupt the quiet but I stay where I am because today, my self-restraint is a gift.

Then, I hear a gate open behind the curtain and I look to see who's behind the talking. An Asian couple, both dressed in perfectly pressed blue jeans and white T-shirts, walks right by me such serious intent I do a double-take. The couple look like husband and wife. They both nod at me and head to a bench overlooking the canal. I get to my feet and follow. Questions tumble over each other in my mouth. I keep quiet as I reach the canal. Standing a fair distance from the couple, I pretend to survey the canal and study two women in their twenties paddling by in a two-seater canoe. I wait. I wait. I need to hear the Asian couple continue a conversation that began behind a curtain. Finally, they resume their dialogue and they sound like any couple on equal footing. She is calm, deliberate and confident. The boy in the man has disappeared. The man sounds mature, articulate and self-assured.

What happened in that garden? Did the boy get left behind and then emerge as a full-grown man? Perhaps the garden brings out the boy in the man when both he and his wife discuss the idea of growing. Maybe, he doesn't want the garden to grow as slowly as his wife does and that brings out the boy in him again to demonstrate his point of view. Perhaps his wife just tolerates the boy but prefers the man.

In flawless English, he says to his wife: "If people around me cause resentment, it's usually because the boy in me is not getting what he wants or the other person is not behaving the way I expect." And his wife replies: "That's because the boy depends too much on people, places and things and if things don't go his way, he starts demanding. Maybe it's all about depending and demanding!"

Behind a curtain of ferns and vines, a woman speaks to someone sounding like a boy wearing the skin of a man.

Fixing

What is the ideal?

On their knees, a man and woman, who look so normal they refuse to be described, try to fix the bottom metal flap on the gate to their garden. The flap is bent inward so the gate will not close properly. Each of them takes a turn trying to pull on the flap and then they try it together. They grunt and sweat and pull until their faces are maps of frustration.

Each of them stands and takes a break while the other tries the claw of a hammer or a piece of two-by-four. Are they trying to shield their perfect garden?

Clean and organized, like a tiny laboratory, the garden looks as if it were dropped out of the sky, perhaps originating from a faraway science lab. White steel trays half-filled with soil sit on metal tables and gleam in the sunlight. What are they planning for these trays? Snow-white bricks are laid perfectly as a floor. Hanging from two walls of their garden are small steel cabinets filled with hidden essentials.

The man stops and pulls out a cellphone from his jean pocket. He calls one person, a second person and even a third. Within a half hour, five people show up, all of whom are younger than the couple and who may be relatives. Someone tries a large screwdriver. Another uses a larger hammer claw. Still the gate will not close completely. The seven of them stand in a circle and discuss possible solutions, as if the entire pathway will slip into the canal if the bent metal flap is not solved soon. Later, someone walks to his vehicle and returns with a crowbar. He hands the crowbar to the woman and she quite easily bends the metal flap back to where it should nearly be. She tries the gate and it almost closes perfectly. However, this is not good enough for the husband and he grabs the crowbar from his wife's hands. Then he forces the crowbar behind the metal flap and pulls it towards him. Still the garden gate does not close completely. He drops the crowbar to the ground and asks everyone to follow him to the bench. There each member of the group shows increasing levels of irritation until the woman shouts: "All of you…stop! It's good enough for me!"

Moving away from the group, she walks back to the gate and opens and closes it with enough ease. "Have a look at this," she says.

Others throw up their palms to the glaring sun and seem to ask why she is satisfied with an imperfect gate.

The woman opens and closes the gate one more time and smiles. Her husband's face is stone-wrinkled. When he attempts to pick up the crowbar again, the woman yells: "Just… leave… it… alone!"

When he asks her why, his wife answers with arms swinging round and round, like the hands of an out-of-control clock: "Don't you get it? The gate is good enough!"

"For you maybe," the husband replies. "Doesn't every garden have a life of its own that needs protecting?"

"Maybe, but do you want to stand guard here forever? Do you? Your kind of thinking has no end to it!"

What is the ideal?

Arms

THERE IS ONE WILL IN ALL OF THIS.

A young Filipino couple sits a couple of elbows away from each other on a bench near a bare garden. The boy flaps his forearms in the air, like an orchestra conductor and tries to move as close as possible to the girl. In turn, she flaps her own forearms back at him resisting his advances. Then he tries forcing his face onto hers and her head becomes a metronome trying to avoid his hungry mouth. Then their soup-bone arms flail and the empty garden almost sighs in the afternoon heat, as if it is bored.

The girl then slides to the end of the bench and the boy moves with her. More flailing follows until the girl stands and stabs her righteous index finger at him for being what she says is "a bad boy".

"I'm not a bad boy," he exclaims, his bottom lip protruding over his chin. "My mother knows me. She reminds me that I'm a good boy!"

"Your mother's not here to watch her 'good boy' in action and… be careful you don't trip over your bottom lip," the girl replies. "Someone might be watching."

The boy stands at least an arm's length from her and they both move closer to the empty garden. Grabbing onto the wire mesh fencing, the boy sucks in the bottom of his mouth and asks: "Why is there nothing growing in this garden?"

"Maybe there is but we can't see anything yet," the girl says.

"And why are you always so right?" the boy asks.

"Because you don't know right from wrong," she answers puffing her mouth at the sun.

The boy moves closer to her making sure to keep his flapping to himself.

"Something's wrong with that garden," he says. "I don't think anything will grow there. Usually, you can see tiny, green shoots sticking out of the soil or at least… something close to that anyway."

By this time the boy stands almost hip-to-hip with the girl, his hands tucked firmly into the back pockets of his jeans… just in case. Moving up and down on her toes, the girl turns her head and quickly checks for the location of his hands and she notices the boy's knuckles protruding.

"Do you think your hands have a future?" she asks.

"What kind of question is that?" he replies, the furrow deepening between his eyes.

"What are you planning for your career?"

"I don't know yet. It's too early," he replies.

"It's never too soon."

"What's the rush? My mother told me to take my time. I might change careers three times. Hey, maybe that's what the garden is doing…taking its time."

At that point, the knuckles in his back pockets disappear and he moves away from her.

Meanwhile, she remains fascinated with the barren plot.

Soon the boy is walking further away from her, hands perfectly flat in his back pockets. The boy's face is wooden. Desire is long gone.

Moving westward along the canal, the boy withdraws his hands from his jean pockets and swings both arms in widening hoops, as if he were expelling rejection from his body. Breaking into a full run, his arms then swing wildly until they become rope-like in the light of a sudden truth.

There is one will in all of this.

Tongues

THE WOMAN KNOWS WHAT I NEED.

A middle-aged woman with a long, grey pigtail, stops by the grassy hill where I sit.

"How are you today?" she asks, her voice wrapped in even tone. "I see you here most mornings."

"Just about fine," I reply somewhat surprised by her question.

"Why are you just about fine?"

Right then and there I regret prefacing my reply.

"I'm a bit low on energy from maybe saying too much the last few days."

"Is that so? In that case, let me speak."

My eyes turn towards the canal which moves like lava. I take a deep breath and let myself be taken along with the current. Everything inside me slows down to a crawl as I look back towards the woman. Waiting for the right moment to continue, she hasn't taken her eyes off me. My lips seal themselves as I tilt my head slightly to the right which she takes as a sign to say something.

"This may help, and I hope you don't mind, but… I should tell you about what happened to my boyfriend. He had Cancer in his mouth and had a portion of his tongue taken out. Doctors removed a slab of skin from under his right arm and attached it to his tongue. My boyfriend became a new man!"

"What was the biggest change?" I ask.

"Hey, I thought you weren't going to talk! Well, he decided to not open his mouth anymore except to breathe, eat, have sex and answer questions about life or death. He sees no need to open his mouth most times. Friends ask if my boyfriend has speech issues because of the surgery but he is now more articulate than ever."

I'm taking all this in and my hopefully healthy tongue remains curled behind my bottom teeth. I have nothing to say.

"So, what are your thoughts on talking?" she asks. "Your own tongue must be just fine."

I look up at the woman and simply shrug my shoulders indicating that I still have nothing much to say right now. The canal is now almost at a standstill and that makes me quieter than I've been in many days. Becoming a motionless raft on the canal, I watch my words perch on that raft, like children who momentarily stop what they are doing and open their faces to a wall of sun.

"You can talk now," she says. "Your turn."

I'm still speechless and I point to the canal. The woman turns her head and studies the water. "It's my own tongue," I finally say. "One minute my tongue has to be the centre of attention and the next it wants to hide because it feels worthless. Perhaps my tongue is addicted to something, maybe words."

"But… at least it works," the woman replies. "You sure sound eloquent to me."

"Thank you. No Cancer so far. My tongue can be obsessed with words and conversations can become allergies for my body, sometimes resulting in a rash. Maybe I'm delusional and swallow my tongue when I think I'm telling the truth."

The woman knows what I need.

After Thirty-Five Years

I SAY NOTHING AND LOOK FOR MORE BIRDS.

A woman, who might be on the early side of fifty, has long curly hair the colour of mahogany. She's dressed in washed out sweat pants, a cream-coloured T-shirt and cherry-red flip-flop sandals. On her forehead, just above her nose, is a bunched-up, thimbleful of skin that looks like a small accordion between her green eyes. In her right hand she carries a whiter than white Styrofoam cup of coffee. In her left hand she twirls a black baseball cap at the end of her index finger. While doing her canal dance, the woman moves her lips up to her eyes as if asking the sky a silent question and then nods at me with large brown-black eyes. Round and round, back and forth she dances not spilling a drop of coffee.

"I've often seen you here by the canal and I've always wanted to talk to you," she says pausing.

"Really? Why thank you," I reply sitting up on the canal bench. "I've seen you around here too," I say.

"Hope you don't mind," she says. "If I tell you but my mother and father got back together thirty-five years of being apart. The day they broke up, my parents sent me to live with my aunt. I haven't seen them in all that time. When I found out they were back together, I tracked them down. Imagine, they asked me who I was because it had been so long. To learn about me all over again will take time."

Still twirling her baseball cap, the woman squats on the grass and sips from her coffee cup.

"Do you think I'm odd?" she asks, her cap still spinning on her finger.

"No, I have my own quirks too," I reply shrugging my shoulders.

"Did you like my canal dancing?"

"Very much. I was also very curious about what you're planning to do about your parents"

"I'm asking myself how to start all over again because I don't have a clue," she says.

"Why are you even thinking about doing that…especially since they left you and you were the one who tracked them down? How could they forget about you? Were they at least glad to hear from you?" I ask with a quizzical look on my face.

"They were stunned," replies the woman, her baseball cap still spinning on her index finger. "Thirty-five years is a long time."

Two pigeons on the canal wall peck at each other's chests and then eye one other with a dream-like fondness. The birds could be the main characters in a TV ad trying to sell the newest smartphone or online dating website and using the intimacy of pigeons to make their pitch. Or perhaps their pigeon love is brand new and the chemistry between them is much more than infatuation. Maybe the two birds simply haven't seen each other for years and they're making up for lost time.

Both of us stop talking and quietly study the two pigeons. Occasionally, they flap their wings excitedly at each other, their claws jittering from side to side. An enormous grey cloud, the shape of a gigantic duvet, covers the sun. Will the sunless sky make a difference? The temperature drops. The wind picks up. Looking away from each other, the pigeons separate. With their backs to one other, each bird takes three or four steps in opposite directions and then take off over the canal.

"The older I get, the less I know about relationships," I tell the woman.

"Maybe my parents are nothing more than pigeons," she says, her baseball cap now scrunched up in her hand.

I say nothing and look for more birds.

Canal Hearts

A DISCOVERY CAN BE DIFFICULT TO MEASURE.

The woman strolling by sees me reading a novel and stops. The way she stands and almost opens her arms to me tells me that her own story will be an incoming wave about to crash on my bench.

"I am afraid of books yet I belong to a book club," she says. "I hardly ever read the books but I really enjoy the company of people in the club," she adds. "But I sure hope my daughter doesn't become like me."

All of this is so sudden; I must have a neon sign blinking on my forehead that reads "OPEN".

Once after reading a book of fiction that included a very rare violent incident, the woman refused to travel to that location ever again, whether day or night. Both she and her daughter also suffer from depression and she tries everything to keep them both out of that wet paper bag.

"I have to protect myself from stories," she says. "Some of them are dangerous."

"What do you mean?" I ask.

"I identify emotionally with everything I read. I can't help it. Doesn't matter what kind of story. Even if someone wrote stories…say about this canal, I'd worry," she replies, her face animated with fear.

"What about your daughter?"

"I hadn't wanted any babies but it didn't take too long for me to love her."

"So how do you survive?" I ask.

"I grew a shell around my heart and kept my daughter inside it."

I stand and look down into the canal and see fish of various sizes gravitate to what looks like a huge chunk of white bread but then swim quickly away before devouring it. Do the fish know something I don't? A flat white fish approaches, forms a platform under the bread, and then swims off without touching it. Usually, pieces of bread only float for seconds and then they either sink or are eaten by fish. Not today. This large lump of bread is going nowhere.

"Do you think that piece of bread in the water has a hard heart?" I ask the woman pointing to the canal. But the woman doesn't answer. Instead, she turns completely away from me and slowly slides her feet to the edge of the canal.

"That bread must be stale and hard as marble," she says.

"Still, sooner or later, shouldn't it turn soggy and sink to the bottom? What's keeping it afloat?" I ask.

The woman picks up a stick and aims it at the bread. The stick hits the bread and sinks. The bread just bobs across the water, its whiteness flashing in the light, like a small patch of lost stars. She tries stones of various sizes and different items, including a battered shoe from the trash can. Nothing works. Then I picture her lunging into the canal to either force the bread under or retrieve it. Instead, she throws up her hands.

"Okay, okay you win! There's no way am I'm going to jump into that filthy water over a slice of bread."

I can't believe my ears and I wonder if the woman's heart can float on its own.

Soon she turns back towards me and watches me engrossed in my novel again.

"Aren't you ever afraid that your story will devour you?" she asks.

"Actually, I enjoy being eaten alive by a good story," I say.

A discovery can be difficult to measure.

Holy Darkness

Nothing seems gradual.

Today the sun drops cleanly, as a giant orange disc, behind a line of the sky.

A couple in their late forty's, must understand the quickness of these sunsets from what looks like another secret get-together. On the bench they both check over their own shoulders, as if they are making sure their own spouses are nowhere to be seen. They wait for the sudden dusk to vanish so they can cover each other with their own heat. As long as the lights are almost out, this couple looks like they could be intimate, even in the branches of a darkened tree.

Perhaps, the last time they made love was in an empty church kitchen. They were attending a going away party on the roof of the church's rectory. Cases of beer, numerous liquor bottles and intriguing containers of wine were everywhere. While their spouses were up on the roof chatting harmlessly together, the lovers were heaving against each other on the kitchen counter, just below the roof in full view of only a ceiling fan eye. The couple emerged from the kitchen, one… thirty seconds after the other and their skins delicious with the taste of booze and kitchen counter sex.

A spritely woman, close to seventy, out walking her dog, approaches their bench and smiles at the lovers after they have released one other.

"I want to get my walk done as soon as possible because those damn rats are huge and now's the time they come out to feed," she says. "And my dog is so small."

"Good idea," the couple say at almost the same time. "So you better keep moving."

Now the two are alone, wrapped in a blanket of night and the canal pathway looks and sounds empty.

"We should get a room," the woman says.

"Yeah, sure, a room," he says.

"But that wouldn't be right," she says, her face looking too full for a confessional.

"True. That would be real cheating on our spouses."

"We've never rented a room before."

"We've never had to," he says.

"Remember the kitchen counter sex we had at the going away roof party in that church?"

"I'll never forget it," she says, her smile reaching up to her eyes.

"And we didn't need to rent a room," she says. "I love church sex, the wicked side of joy, the thrill."

"Remember… all religions are institutions and institutions are made up of people and people are… fallible. They mess up," says the man.

"You sound like one of those curb-side preachers. Look, a bunch of those gray, four-legged flaws are heading our way. Time to go," she says, as if each and every rat might be a sin.

"Where to?"

"There's sure to be an empty church somewhere." she laughs lightly tracing an index finger on his face.

Nothing seems gradual.

From Disowned to Owned

SPECULATION CAN BE FOUND ANYWHERE.

In a breakfast café on the boulevard just south of the canal, the young waitress serves me a plate of scrambled eggs, sausages and a bowl of pineapple, papaya, mango and melon. With eyes and long-stringy hair the colour of soil, she reaches straight up to the morning sky with her tallness. So perfectly tanned is her face she could sell sunscreen for Walmart.

I make sure I look straight at her face when requesting my order and am very grateful for her effort. I promise myself to leave a generous tip because she is both efficient and friendly. Also, most waitresses I have encountered work very hard and are perhaps not appreciated.

Business is slow this morning so the waitress has time to talk.

"How are you today?" I ask between mouthfuls.

"A bit scared," she says standing near my table and wringing her hands.

"Oh, and... why is that?"

"I'm going home soon for the first time in seven years."

She ran away from home at sixteen with only a backpack and enough money for a one-way ticket. Her parents disowned her and now at twenty-three, she is heading home.

"May I ask why you left in the first place?"

"My father and I couldn't stand each other. Maybe it all came from his sperm when I was conceived. What did it though was one night I happened to be downtown shopping with a friend and I spotted him cuddling with a younger women in the window of a downtown coffee shop. Even after I told my mother, she wouldn't believe me. Because of my truth, they both denied that I was their daughter and wanted nothing more to do with me. So, I took them at their word and ran away the next day when I pretended to leave for school. I've been doing mostly waitressing the last seven years."

Then, she tells me of the many uncertainties, the main one being: how does she change from being disowned? For seven years this young woman has not been owned by anyone except maybe a couple of shady restaurant owners who treated her like she was their property so she didn't last long in those jobs.

"I belong to nobody but me," she says. "It might be difficult for my parents too. Another customer once told me that belonging to no one is safer. There's no investment that way. More coffee?"

"Sure. Why not," I reply holding my cup as she poured. "But who's invested in whom?"

"Yeah, I think I've forgotten what I have sunk into my parents."

"How do you measure something like that?" I ask.

"Well, I guess I'll find out soon enough, won't I? It's so much easier figuring out how much money I have in my savings account."

"For sure, but what does your own savings account have to do with your mother and father?"

"My parents were always big savers...in lots of ways," the waitress says. "I learned that from them."

"Then maybe... just maybe...they have been saving up something, whatever that may be ... for you and... you have nothing to worry about," I say.

Speculation can be found anywhere.

Counting

"DON'T JUMP!" A PASSING WOMAN YELLS AS SHE DROPS HER SHOPPING bags on the sidewalk.

I turn around on the bench and see several other people joining the woman. Each one offers his or her "don't jump" appeal until everyone chants in unison with their hands held palms upward, like five-fingered pleas.

Up on my feet, I cross the boulevard to find out what's going on.

A man on the late side of forty, dressed in a red and green, Magnum P.I Hawaiian shirt and khaki shorts stands barefooted on the ledge of the third floor of a four story apartment building on the boulevard.

"I'm counting the total number of palms," the man shouts down to the sidewalk. "And when I get to the number I want, I'll think about climbing back inside."

"How many…how many will it take?" someone says in a pleading voice.

"Not sure yet," yells the man on the ledge.

The five men and women stop passersby and ask them to join their group. In no time, there are at least twenty people standing there with their palms open to the sky pleading with the man on the ledge.

Soon the police arrive and later a fire-truck. Two television station vehicles are parked across the street and cameras are pointed upward. A white and blue station-wagon from a local radio station pulls up to the curb and is directed by a police officer to park along the canal. There must be at least thirty people standing on the sidewalk now with their hands held out and palms facing the man, like offerings. Drivers of vehicles moving slowly down the boulevard are unsure what to do, their braking, accelerating, like a jagged ballet.

"Don't jump. Don't jump," the growing crowd chants again and again.

Watching the man point below to the maze of palms, I see how carefully he counts each open hand. I'm amazed at his precision.

"I see forty-two pairs of hands!" the man yells down at us. "But I need more!"

"How many?" a policeman asks.

"At least fifty pairs of hands."

"Why is that?" a reporter cries out.

"I want to be able to count to at least one hundred hands and that will tell me what I need to know."

Everyone in the crowd including policemen, firemen and media people pull out their cellphones inviting many more hands.

"We need help. We need more hands or this guy will jump," voices say.

Within a half hour the entire sidewalk is jammed with spectators all holding their hands, palms stretched to the sky, as if each finger were a devotion of sorts.

"Let me count!" the man hollers down to the sidewalk and then places his right index finger over his lips. "Quiet everyone... QUIET, please! Let me count. My life depends on it."

The crowded sidewalk becomes so silent with all lips forming intersessions. Next, one of the spectators cracks his knuckles and then slowly raises his fingers, one at a time, to the man on the ledge, as if all palms and pleas have the same purpose...one finger at a time.

Same Woman

Two men in their mid-forties cautiously paddle their canoe under the noonday sun.

Each man looks back and forth at each other, as if both are in love with the same woman and are wondering if each man knows about the other.

The second man at the back of the canoe looks uneasy because his frown has turned into the tightest of knots. The first man may be planning to suddenly turn and smack the second man across the head with his paddle. Dumping the body right there in the canal might be easy under one of the bridges where darkness and depth can fool anyone. Then he'd paddle back to his vehicle as quickly as possible and drive somewhere to create an alibi.

Perhaps the first man will go visit his older sister and make sure that she will tell everyone that he arrived at least one hour before the real time on her kitchen clock. She's the kind of sister who would take a bullet for him because she understands his passion. After that, he will phone the woman both men love and make dinner plans with her for the evening.

The second man in the front of the canoe is also concerned. Just as easily, the second man could use his own paddle to slam the first man in the back of the head and his life would be over. Perhaps the second man might realize that the water level is too low to simply drop the dead body into the canal, even under a darkened bridge. He may carry the body, wrapped in a blanket, to his car and stuff it into his trunk. Then he'd drive to an isolated windy field, drag the body across the dirt, dig a grave and dump the body into the blackness. Hopefully the blowing sand and dirt will cover up the rest. Driving back to town, he would stop at the side of the road and call that woman. He might tell her that he's absolutely sure he's the only man who truly loves her and that he'll pick her up shortly after six so they can watch the sun lose itself behind the sky.

On the other hand, the woman is accustomed to having more than one man in her life at the same time. Perhaps, according to horoscope experts, she is a Gemini, making it impossible for her to do otherwise, as if horoscopes were at the heart of all motives. The woman has always had at least two men in her life and each of those men felt that he was her only lover. She constantly tells her woman friends that if they think the only way to a man's heart is through his stomach, then they are aiming far too high. Or, if they try to focus on a man's brain, there might be nothing there but a vast arid region.

Her lovers are allowed to do most of the talking and they do. They talk about their jobs, their accomplishments and their money. If the men are tall or short they talk about how being tall or short sometimes gives them power. Occasionally, her lovers go on and on reinventing cliches about how they are not getting enough loving at home and that's when the woman asks for more details. Often, the men explain how they aren't allowed any down time, especially when they first come home from work, as if down time had anything to do with gender, even if both husband and wife return from work at the same time. Meanwhile, she listens to every word, as if each syllable is a gulp of oxygen needed for her survival. After the men leave, the woman becomes the main character in a TV sitcom floating through her days and giggling into the ear of televised life.

The two distressed men in the canoe disappear under yet another bridge. When they finally emerge on the other side, the canoe is empty and drifts past a man in his early twenties who is fishing. Right away, the fisherman spots the unoccupied canoe and his curiosity takes over. Struggling to reel in his catch, his fishing line snaps and forms a huge… loopy question mark in the air.

I Had No Choice for My Hair Colour

"And the woman replies, "Watch this."

An elderly woman with eggshell-white hair and the nose of a hawk is loudly interacting with a couple of men about the same age as she is. Both men have monk-like shaved heads with grey fringes of hair. Everyone is re-loading their guns and the intensity is what keeps them on their feet.

"I think women are tougher on each other than men are," the first man says.

"No way," the woman insists stabbing the man in his chest with her right index finger. "I raised four sons, one of whom was adopted. They were ruthless, especially with my adopted boy. By the way, I took on that boy to give back because I too was adopted."

"Good for you but I worked mostly with women," the first man adds. Felt like days in a shark tank."

"See this white hair of mine? It used to be dark brown. I'd kill for those four boys of mine but each one of them could be a piece of work," she says.

The air becomes bluer and the ferocity is off the scale. People walking by give the three lots of space. Even dogs on leashes refuse to walk in a straight line past the three debaters. After a pause in the gender breathing, the woman bends over to pick up a Frisbee that has landed by her feet. Almost immediately, a teen-age boy runs up to her gasping and thanks the woman. Words stop flying among the three adults and that allows them to sit on the bench.

"Now, where were we?" the second man asks.

"Yeah, I was telling you about my adopted son. He sure had to toughen up and fight his own battles. Or so I thought. About three years ago, at twenty-eight, he ended his own life. On that day, I stopped dying my hair. The colour made me feel guilty. Just three days after his passing, I received a letter in the mail from him telling me that he's gay."

Like a curtain on a stage, even the murmuring becomes utter speechlessness. The two men try to say something but their mouths are glued shut. People walking by sense the reverence of the moment and they lower their heads. Unsure winds are probably parked behind mountain clouds or off chasing each other across the blue. Even the sun has toned down its radiance and three clouds huddle, like anxious children in a sky corner…waiting…waiting.

"I had no choice for my hair colour," the woman finally says. "Really!"

"Sorry to hear about your adopted boy," the first man offers with his own head partially lowered. "I've read that some gay men take their own lives."

"Doesn't matter who's tougher, eh," says the second man looking straight at the woman. "But you know, and this is me being word for word honest, I really like your classy white hair. It's a nice contrast with those remarkable brown eyes… truthful… bright…alive! You give off light! Wish I could say that about my own eyes."

"Me too," says the second man.

"Thank you, guys. When I now look at myself in the mirror, I sometimes blame my previously brown hair for not allowing me to see the truth, inside my son. Maybe I was too busy taking care of myself. After my boy died, I let my hair grow out into the honesty of white. Felt like I had to take breathing lessons from my other sons because they knew all along."

"Want to show us how you did that?" the second man asks. "Use me as your mirror if you wish."

And the woman replies, "Watch this."

Water Prayers

It is mid-morning, just before the sun absolutely floods the canal.

Two boys who could be brothers in shorts and T-shirts stand calmly under sprinklers watering the grass, as if they are taking a sun shower.

The first boy wearing bottle-green shorts and a bright yellow T-shirt has longish hair that half-covers his ears. Holding his hands to his face to keep the water from entering his eyes, he peeks out from behind his fingers and checks on his younger brother.

The younger boy, wearing pale-blue shorts and a white T-shirt has much shorter hair, and both of his hands are stretched out and facing upward. His fingers try to trap the water and he is almost hypnotized by his efforts. Are the boys playing or praying?

Meanwhile, right by the canal, their mother and father, both dressed in dark blue from head-to-toe, may be writing spiritual requests on slips of paper and then flinging them up into the air, watch them float over the canal and then land on the water, like wafers of humility. What are they doing?

They have many plastic Safeway bags already stuffed with completed slips so their petitions might last for some time. When their first bag of requests settles on the canal water, the current seems to slow down and swallows one prayer at a time. Some slips of paper take longer to sink and they may contain concerns that can't be addressed right away. Or maybe the couple are not ready yet for any answer. These replies might say: "WAIT". The prayers that sink easily may have replies that say: "YES" or "NO".

Are they re-inventing their spirituality? The couple could be saying to each other that perhaps religions are for those who are afraid to go to Hell but they have been to Hell and don't want to go back. Maybe the woman had so much difficulty getting pregnant, that she knows all about Hell and is grateful to have given birth to two healthy sons. And her husband might be so thankful, he would have found a way to give birth to their two boys himself-ifthat were possible. Spiritual requests for them seem to be far more than a duty.

Back under the sprinklers, the two boys haven't moved. The timed sprinklers are now spraying more water on them, as if the sprinklers are preparing the boys for a new ritual. Both boys are simply staring up at the sky and letting the water wash over them. Then their mother's voice instructs them to fold their hands together in a pious way and the sons do as they are told. With eyes closed and heads bowed, the boys fall to their knees and move their lips in a silent shower of devotion.

The parents fling two more Safeway prayer bags over the canal. Right away, mother and father also fall to their knees to make this place a complete outdoor house of worship. There is no priest, minister or rabbi. Nobody is dressed in their Sunday best on this Wednesday morning. No pulpit. No one is preaching or requesting money. No choir or hymns. There are only four members in this congregation. Extending quiet wishes to the family are armfuls of generous sunlight. This may be a celebration of water, of light and the easy way water and sun understand acceptance.

On their feet, each grabbing the remaining Safeway prayer bags, they give a final fling. Then the family bows empty-handed at the passing current. No one needs a burning bush to appear or a white mist to cover the canal No one looks disappointed, as if they all have no expectations, no dependencies and no demands… in their own immaterial world.

It is mid-morning, just before the sun floods the canal.

Cement Changes

On the middle cement step down to the canal, the grandmother cradles an infant in her left arm. Dressed in a head-to-toe, tomato-red pyjama outfit, the child is partially wrapped in a white woollen blanket. It is only seven in the morning and the woman unfolds the child to its first rays of early sunshine, as if offering the baby to the highest of all powers.

"My daughter needed a break and so I decided to bring my new granddaughter down to the canal." she says to me.

Dressed in a royal-blue light jacket, white blouse and pale blue pants, the grandmother makes faces at the baby hoping to get some kind of response. Her long hair, tied back in two pigtails, swings back and forth with each new facial expression. But the infant just stares quietly at the grandmother and may not be ready for smiling. Then the grandma moves the child to her right arm so she can scratch an itchy right shoulder with her left hand.

"Hello. Do you like babies?" she asks looking up at me on the top step. "My name is Mona and the infant's name is Patricia."

"I'm Ken," I say. "Yes, I do like babies, Mona, but mostly because I am curious about all the 'firsts' they do like opening their eyes or watching how they respond to certain stimuli, like how you were trying to make Patricia react to your funny faces. Looks like she's not quite ready yet."

"Yes, let's give her more time to smile. But I sure hope this child isn't like her mother who took herself far too seriously from the day she came into the world. Yes, my daughter was born wearing a cement diaper and she's still like that."

"I suppose everyone develops a personality of their own eh, Mona," I say.

"To tell you the truth, I think my own daughter's personality was pre-formed inside my womb from the time she was conceived. She never laughed at anything and rarely does now at twenty-eight. She hardly ever cries or shows any feelings."

"Is she depressed? Are you or your husband like that? Maybe sometimes it's genetic."

"No, both my husband and I love to laugh and we certainly don't keep our emotions locked up so I don't know what to think. I sure hope this baby girl doesn't become like her mother."

The grandmother faces the child directly and again tries to roll her eyes and bend and twist her face and even tickle the infant's belly. Suddenly, Patricia's mouth shows a slight curl on the corners so the grandma continues until the curl widens and moves up towards the baby's ears. "She's done it!"

"She sure has. Good work," I say.

"What a relief! You wouldn't believe what we tried to do with our daughter."

"Bet you can't wait to get Patricia back to her mom so you can tell her what happened."

"I'm not so sure about that."

"Why? Maybe your daughter might surprise you and be delighted."

"Hard to say," Mona replies. "You know how my daughter is."

"No… not really," I answer.

On the middle cement step down to the canal, the grandmother cradles an infant in her left arm.

The Suitcase

FIVE PIGEONS ARE PERCHED ON A BLOOD-RED SUITCASE.

Blue-gray ripples of water surround the birds and the travel bag. There are no labels or tags attached to the luggage. Also, three floating mysterious shapes the size of human heads bob up and down near the suitcase.

One bird with a marble-coloured head and a white tail is half-turned away from the suitcase and has already decided to leave. A second bird struts towards the handle of the luggage, as if ready to open the bag and search for more ownership clues. Two other pigeons, both more grey than white, watch the first bird to see what happens. The fifth pigeon is indifferent, yet remains close by and continues pecking at the luggage in case, just in case.

The three human head shapes could be the faces of past owners. One face might belong to a clown who may have left home at the age of fifteen with the red suitcase half-filled with clothes. The clown's father was starting to dislike circus stories and all this did was make the boy want to leave even more. Later on, the clown passed on the bag to the ringmaster's daughter who quit the circus to become a psychology student at university and her forehead is far bigger than the rest of her head. Eventually, the psychology student passed on the red suitcase to a patient who was being released from a hospital mental ward. This patient's face has an enormous corncob nose and other such unusual facial features that even the pigeons pretend to look elsewhere. After the patient decided that his mental state was only temporary, he heaved the luggage into the canal. An hour later, the man drowned himself in his home aquarium, the fish startled out of their gills and the man's face flushed down the toilet with the fish and later into the canal.

Now the luggage bobs up and down still unopened, looking as if it should be lying on an airport carousel instead. No one claims the bag. The entire carousel is empty except for the bag's redness. Flights have come and gone. Passengers ignore the luggage. The airport shuts down for the night. In the dark, the suitcase lies like a giant red bruise. Surprisingly, no one from Security has removed the red bag and brought it to Lost and Found. A passing cleaning crew member hoists the bag off the carousel and it is heavy. On the floor the suitcase is opened completely. Inside are the lives of three people meticulously folded and packed away with the upmost care: complete clown outfits looking like new, scholarly books filled with absolutes about why people behave like they do and masks that hide the same fears over and over again but expecting different results.

The cleaning crew member closes the suitcase, lifts it onto his trash barrel and rolls everything to the back of the airport and places it outside.

There, the red bag stays in the dark as a noisy a garbage truck makes its rounds. The suitcase is picked out and strapped to the side of the truck, the driver unsure if he will take it all the way to the dump. As the truck moves through the four am darkness along the canal, the driver makes a sudden stop. Unstrapping the suitcase, the driver checks to his right, to his left and then behind him. Finally, he flings the bag into the canal and climbs back into the truck.

Inside the suitcase, three people stop struggling to be themselves and finally accept that they were meant to float together on the endless possibilities of a canal.

Five pigeons are perched on a blood-red suitcase.

Orphan

Lying on its side underwater and coated with mostly green moss, the shopping cart may have at least one more life.

The cart, whose handle has disappeared, still has all four wheels and its steel-ribbed flap in the back is wide open. The largest clumps of moss cling to the corners of the cart and where the wheels meet the frame. The Safeway grocery store sign, still attached to the top flap, is partially covered in rust so the cart could be an orphan, lost for decades.

Perhaps, a homeless woman used the cart to carry everything she owned. One day while sleeping deeply on a bench in the early afternoon, the woman was robbed of all her possessions except for the cart. Wisely, she knew that it was safer to sleep during the day because night-time can be dangerous for homeless people. Yes, the cart became her child but also her home on wheels. Still, her belongings were taken from her. After the realization of her loss, the woman kicked at her empty cart so many times, it eventually fell over on its side, like a beaten animal. Then she picked up the cart, placed it on its wheels and continued her kicking. Finally, the woman pushed the empty cart into the canal and resumed her loner life.

Or, the cart was shoved into the canal after an aging bottle and can picker had just about run out of energy and had done his last load. He knew that he was headed for long-term stay…somewhere under a bridge. From years of experience, the man knew that money made from bottles and cans did not keep up with the cost of living. For a long time, he had meticulously recorded everything before going to the depot with his packed cart to make sure he got every penny. On one occasion, the person behind the counter gave him less cash than he expected and he made so much of a fuss that he was paid exactly what he expected. His last few visits to the depot always began with him telling them precisely how much money he had in his cart and they believed him. Leaving his fate to the unknown, maybe he was that child who was dropped off at a zoo many years ago and left there abandoned.

Today, I look down into the canal and see the shopping cart's steel ribs as my own ribs. I recall as a boy walking at night in front of a display window of a huge glass and paint company during a howling Montreal snowstorm. Inside the window were various types and sizes of mirrors for sale. I remember my skin feeling like it hung on the body of an outcast as the hollow winter wind blew right through me. The more I looked into the different mirrors, the more isolated I felt. I even forgot where I was born. The bones attached to my spine were frozen. Outside the display window were clumps of bushes half-covered in snow and I wanted to lie down and sleep there for as long as it took for my skin to feel right. The bushes seemed to welcome the overwhelming waif going nowhere inside me. But with one more life in me, like the shopping cart, I was determined to fit into the world… somewhere.

Fish of various sizes now swim casually through the cart's bones. Perhaps they see the moss and steel as nothing more than normal life in the canal. The fish don't need the cart for their belongings or even for empty bottles and cans. Although the fish live in their own perpetual orphanage, they may not know any better because their notion of family comes and goes.

Lying on its side underwater and coated with mostly green moss, the shopping cart has at least one more life.

The Lawn Chair

NO CHAIR SHOULD REMAIN AT THE BOTTOM OF A CANAL ALL TWISTED in pain, its purpose lost…even if the agony is imagined.

Like a tangled, silver colon, the lawn chair lies at the bottom of the canal, as if someone had their insides ripped out in the middle of the night and then tossed into the water.

Maybe the chair's life began years ago in a big box-store where a tourist couple decided to purchase two lawn chairs so they could simply sit by the canal and let the world ebb by them through layers of sun and light. Suppose they were litigation lawyers relaxing and celebrating that many of their cases were solved through some sort of mediation and saving money for everyone. After several days of sitting here and at the beach, the lawyer couple flew back home and they left the two chairs on the balcony of their hotel room for the next visitors.

What if the next couple came from Saskatchewan and they just loved their booze and shopping? He worked as an accountant and she was a retired school teacher. Because they were both extremely overweight, each struggled to see where they were heading. Also, their heavy drinking made them fearful of losing everything so the couple brought the two chairs everywhere, including another big-box-store shopping trip.

One afternoon, they forgot one of the chairs against a wall in of a Walmart men's wear department. When they returned for the chair, they checked in LOST AND FOUND and the chair was nowhere to be found…gone. For the remaining portion of their trip, the two decided to share the one chair. Later that day, while resting by the canal, with him lying on the grass and her slumped in the lawn chair, they both fell asleep. Suddenly, the woman's weight broke several of the webbing straps and she toppled onto the grass.

"What happened to you?" the man blurted out startled from his nap.

"Ah, it must be the cheap chair," his wife replied. "Something snapped."

"Are you okay?"

"I'm fine. Think I'll join you on the grass though. But first, I'm going to get rid of this piece of crap."

The woman huffed and puffed herself to her feet and then smashed the chair several times against the cement steps leading down to the water. Then she flung the twisted mess into the canal. The chair sank slowly to the bottom and clouds of dirt rose to the surface, like tiny screens...perhaps the chair's closing act.

All this happened some time ago and today the lawn chair has shaped its own martyrdom there at the bottom of the canal. Maybe, the chair is still writing the story of its life and it hopes to be re-united with the two litigation lawyers. Wouldn't it be wonderful if one of those lawyers could prepare a case against the retired teacher? The woman teacher could be sued for broken bones, possible brain injury, spinal cord concerns, ripped skin, psychological trauma, diminished value and lost days of use. The possibilities are endless. Nobody would dare make jokes such as; "How can you tell when a lawyer is not telling the truth? When his or her lips are moving." No, these lawyers were weaned on integrity and would never poke fun at their own profession. They'd want to know what happened to the chair and might track down the other couple.

No chair should remain at the bottom of a canal all twisted in pain, its purpose lost...even if the agony is imagined.

My Cravings Are All Yours

"But I don't know how my desires began," Solange says.

A man wearing wine-coloured shorts, black runners and a lime-coloured T-shirt, juggles three balls against the blinding eye of an early morning sun. He looks to be just over six feet tall, has the frame of a wire fence and if he turned sideways, he'd vanish. With hair the colour of asphalt and pale skin, his ice-blue eyes are focussed, like lasers, on his juggling. As each ball pauses in mid-air, the canal surface almost snaps a picture of the manipulating.

Also witnessing all this is a bare arm wrapped around a lone tree. It's as if the owner of the bare arm doesn't want to be caught watching too long in case the juggler's balls dropped. The hand at the end of the arm is somewhat wrinkled and is certainly not the arm of a child.

Then the juggler, without dropping a ball, turns from the canal to the tree and asks aloud: "Would the person attached to that arm please identify yourself?"

The arm disappears behind the tree and then two arms appear embracing the same tree. "Are those arms connected to someone?" the juggler asks half-laughing.

A woman appears from behind a tall, aging tree with a horizon grin stitched across her face. She wears a dandelion-yellow T-shirt, snow-white slacks and what looks like brand new, cognac-coloured leather sandals. Her hair, the colour of maple syrup, is tied up in two small buns on top of her head and the woman's eyes are sparkling green in the sunlight. Her face sags slightly and her skin is the colour of dark raisins. When the woman opens her lips to talk, her teeth are so stark-white that her mouth is loud without her having said a word.

"My name is Solange," the woman says.

"Why hide behind that tree, Solange?" the juggler asks.

"I have been watching you for some time and didn't want to distract you."

"No problem. I love having an audience but I really do this juggling to give my brain a workout."

"What do you mean?" Solange asks, her face creased with curiosity.

"The juggling magnifies the pathways to my brain. This helps me solve problems. I've read that it may even prevent Alzheimer's," he says.

"That's something I think about at my age but I have other problems."

"What's that?" the juggler asks.

"Addictions… I have a couple of them including overeating. Sorry if it sounds like I'm dumping on you but I've developed these intense and constant desires. No joke. I'm really worried. Do you think juggling would help?"

"Anything's possible, Solange," replies the juggler. "I've only read that juggling may remove strong urges for junk foods, like potato chips but I'm not sure about other foods. Anything's possible though."

For the next couple of hours, the man teaches Solange how to juggle…one ball…two balls…three.

"Try to make sure that each ball rises to the eye or chin level," he tells her.

Solange practices and practices often dropping several balls but eventually she starts to get it.

"You learn fast. Come back tomorrow and we'll work at it together," he says. "Those powerful urgings are like an allergy of the body, an obsession of the mind… an intense, constant hunger. I have my own cravings too."

"But I don't know how my desires began," Solange says.

Bathtubs and Smiles

STANDING UP STRAIGHT IN THE NEAR END OF DAYLIGHT, I WALK AWAY from my illusionary search for the perfect canal smile because the smile has found me.

An imaginary larger body of water at the far end of the canal looks as if it is splashing up the sky. Is this the inside of a bathtub being filled or emptied?

Nearby, a man with a gleaming bald head and a woman, both perhaps in their mid-fifties, speak French to each other with such passion, their heat could cause the canal to evaporate. She is about a head taller than the man and is dressed in various blues from head-to-toe. Her eyes are the colour of lust.

"Tu es trop belle!" he says looking up to her. "Too beautiful."

"Toi aussi, she replies tucking her long, grey-streaked, chestnut hair back behind her ears. "You too."

When they see the imaginary water sloshing up to the sky, they immediately stop talking, stand on the grass above the path and pretend they are bathing each other in the wet warmth of the sun. Their hands are a small dance barely touching each other's hair, face and arms. Because of their actions, the sunset over to their left, brightens as it sets buildings on fire.

Then they talk about how one bathtub is a perfect fit for both of them.

"We'll go slow and easy just like that big body of water and the sky," the woman says. "I'll go home right now and get everything ready. We can eat later."

"Sure. I'll pick up something for supper," he says. No cooking for us tonight. Mind if I just sit here awhile longer? I want to enjoy what that big water does to the sky."

"Of course. See you later," replies the woman.

The man's eyes are fixed on the bathtub sky. As I walk by, his eyes turn to me and his greeting comes out of a mouth in great need of dental work but his smile doesn't care.

"Bonjour," he says.

Dressed in a fresh, pink T-shirt that hangs over his belly, like a small drape, followed by light brown shorts and light brown sandals, the man looks as if he were born with confident bones. Facing the canal, he sits with his arms outstretched in gratitude. His huge brown eyes belong to either a boy in a Van Gogh painting or a Disney cartoon character.

From the crooked darkness in his mouth, the man says: "What a beauty of a day!"

Maybe dental decay and allure naturally belong in the same place.

And perhaps they do both belong together in a bathtub. Rotting teeth may be the product of questionable oral hygiene but contemplating a bath with a loved one is more important right now.

Although I try to hide my staring, the man is quick to close his lips.

"Do you see how that water splashes up against the sky?"

"Oui," the man replies. "I see it. That's what my lover and I were talking about earlier."

"Do you think our eyes are playing tricks on us?" I ask.

"Could be. The skyline is not where we think it is. Doesn't matter though. My woman and I will still take a bath together later. In our tub, the sun never sets."

As he waits for my response, the man's mouth becomes a wide-open, dark pit, as if joy need not always be bright or white or pure. His anticipation is more than enough.

Standing up straight in the near end of daylight, I walk away from my illusionary search for the perfect canal smile because the smile has found me.

Lilac Woman

THE WOMAN'S SHOUTING IS EASIER ON MY EARS THAN THE SOUND OF her body plunging into today's merciless canal.

A WOMAN ON THE EARLY SIDE OF SIXTY, WITH A SHAVED HEAD and dressed entirely in lilac robes, stands with one foot on the boulevard and another on the grass. An ultra-thin lilac veil partially covers her face as she holds an open can of Diet Sprite out in front of her as an offering to the morning light. She talks and talks only to herself.

"I won't argue with you," she says. "To solve my difficulty I have to take a hard look at my money. I know the answer is there somewhere. Yes, my financial advisor will figure it all out. No, he won't. Yes, he will. Who can I trust? It's certainly not my advisor as he probably makes more in fees than I do with my investments. He tells me to think long-term but he's probably robbing me blind."

Then the woman moves slowly onto the grass and steps carefully down to the edge of the canal, still with the Diet Sprite can held out in front of her.

"What more can I do? What more can I do?" she yells, flinging the can into the water. Has the canal become a mentor or scapegoat for her? With her hands on her hips, the lilac woman wants answers. Now! Because of her intensity, the woman may not know what "yes" and "no" means.

"If you think, I'm going to jump into that water in order to get an answer from you, then you're nuts! Maybe you have all the answers but you are also a cesspool. So tell me, what are you doing about your own polluted life? I can tell you've been robbed blind too, she says to the canal"

Yet, the water lips remain closed. The canal may want to respond but the current is suddenly in a hurry. Even if the water slows down, the woman in lilac may not allow the canal time to reply so she waits muttering to herself, her veil now totally pushed back from her face.

"Do you need help?" I ask.

"Yes…I do. No…I don't," she answers turning her head towards me.

"Can I phone someone for you?"

"Maybe. Have you ever been robbed blind?"

"You mean like the canal which used to have clear stream water running through it?"

"Yes, that's exactly what I mean," she says.

"Well, my own life hasn't exactly been pure and I've probably robbed myself blind on occasion."

"But the canal didn't pollute itself," she reminds me.

"True."

"Also, I don't know if I can trust my financial advisor anymore."

"Then try a new one," I suggest.

"But how do I know if I can rely on any new person when I can't even trust myself?" the woman asks.

"Don't know but I have to go now," I say eyeing my watch. "I have something to do."

"Oh yeah, there you go running off to some make-believe appointment and leaving me alone."

I offer my hands in surrender over my head and then shrug.

"I really have to go."

I turn and move away from her desperation.

The woman's shouting is easier on my ears than the sound of her body plunging into today's merciless canal.

Even the Homeless

After the handshakes, cellphones disappear and the boys' faces are lowered in gratitude, as if they knew they'd follow him home.

During this past year, the number of homeless tree houses has increased in a wall of trees at the end of the canal. The one original tree house, with a blue, green, red and orange roof, now has a worn, cracked, white, plastic, picket-like gate leaning against a tree and two archaic bicycles parked at its entrance. Stretched out on two branches, is a blue-webbed ancient lawn chair. Next to the chair are three, large plastic buckets probably used for drinking water or washing clothes.

The two most recent tree houses have a simple tent on a home-made wooden platform stretched out across branches, high enough off the ground to keep everyone safe at night. These two newcomers will soon catch up to the original settler.

I imagine each new tree fort becoming bigger and better than the one next door: taller picket fences, newer lawn chairs, and parking for more than one bicycle.

My imagining stops right there when the owner of the original treehouse steps out onto a branch and climbs down to the pathway. The man, in his mid-twenties, has long blonde hair with black roots seeping out of his scalp and he's dressed in soiled white shorts and pale pink T-shirt. His face is hard with hunger. The more his anguish shows in his eyes, the quieter his breathing becomes, as if he has been rehearsing forever how to advertise his needs. In his left hand is a home-made sign which says: "anything would help". The man points to its words when I pass him by.

With his face aimed at the sun, his mouth now pleads quietly for help. Air escaping from his lips seems to be carefully measured.

Then with his sign held high, the man moves down the pathway where three teenage boys ask to take his picture by pointing their cellphones at him. Holding up his right hand, he points to his sign. Next, he pulls out his empty right pocket from his shorts to show the boys that he's broke. The boys move away and discuss how they will pay him. They take far too long for the man and his growling stomach. Soon, the three boys return and show him some foreign currency.

"That won't buy me supper at McDonald's tonight", he says. "I need dollars please!" And he pulls out his only one-dollar bill from his left pocket. "Like this."

The boys dig into their pockets again and each boy gives him two dollars. Because he usually gets only one dollar per photo, the man is delighted.

"Come to my house," he gestures to the boys and he leads them to his tree fort. He invites them onto the main branch of his dwelling but they stay at the front entrance. Shaking his head, the man just shrugs at the boys. Then he poses on the main branch and lets them click away with their cellphones.

"Take more," he says pretending to take pictures of them with an invisible cellphone.

The boys use their cellphones in many, many ways. There's at least one photo of him hugging several of his white plastic buckets. There's another of him using a scoop to fill three cloudy, plastic glasses with water which the boys politely refuse. Finally, he climbs down from the main tree branch and offers a handshake to each boy which is gladly accepted.

After the handshakes, cellphones disappear and the boys' faces are lowered in gratitude, as if they knew they'd follow him home.

A Pee in the Canal

"Is that how your story ends?" I ask.

In the late afternoon, on a bottom step leading down to the canal, a businessman dressed in a dark brown suit, polished black dress shoes, white shirt and a striped tie pulls down his zipper and pees into the canal. A tan-coloured briefcase mostly hides what he's doing on one side. There's nothing homeless about him unless he's the kind of man who dresses up for the day in a stolen suit.

Because they may be intrigued by the sudden splatter of yellow, tiny fish rush to the surface. However, the small fish don't stay long when a much larger fish moves into the area. The larger fish studies the urine hitting the water and then pokes its head out of the canal, as if wondering about the man's warm intrusion. "What do you want, Fish?" the man mutters. Pulling up his zipper, he climbs up the steps to the pathway.

Slumping down onto a bench, he lights up a cigar and unbuttons his suit jacket. His potato-sack belly spills over his belt as he inhales from a cigar almost as big as a sink pipe. The cigar still has a narrow band of shiny reddish-orange wrapping around it near the man's mouth. What comes out of his mouth looks as if it is chewed smoke with teeth marks all over it. I imagine his teeth chomping on the first clump of smoke, rolling it back to his molars and then exhaling everything in bite-sized chunks. Because the man seems so content, his eyes glaze over in the light of day.

In the warm air, the cigar smoke makes shapes of messages the businessman wants to send so he can sound important because he may be struggling with his significance. Behind those messages in large smoky letters might be the story of his life. Was he born with a cigar in his mouth instead of his mother's breast? Is the cigar an extra limb? Did it all begin when he first peed in the bathtub clutching a toy briefcase in one hand and gripping his mother's fingers with the other?

The winds are asleep today so the businessman's story hangs steadily in the sky, its words a portrait of intriguing simplicity.

"I'm only guessing from your story that you come from a lower working-class family," I take a chance saying to him. "No silver spoons in your mouth, eh."

"How do you know? Yes, my father worked in a factory. Got paid by the hour and had nothing to sell but his labour. To cover the dirt, he always wore a gray shirt. And he often drank our grocery money. Both of my parents got married drunk at city hall. However, just because I come from that background doesn't mean I have to stay there."

"How did I know? I guessed. No matter where you go, what you do or buy, you still sound and behave like someone who comes from a lower working-class background. You might be able to coat some of that with education, fancy purchases, extravagant trips but you have to bring you with you wherever you go."

"What are you trying to reply?"

"It's quite apparent," I say.

"Listen, you're disturbing me, mister, so get lost!" he growls biting down on his cigar.

"Well, your story's right there… in your cigar smoke. Take a look," I say.

"Before you go, when's the last time you had a good pee in the canal?" he asks.

"Is that how your story ends? I ask.

My Face is Worth It

WALKING AWAY FROM THE TWO MEN, I LOOK OVER THE WALL AND, half-way down the steps, a spider spins its silken threads with the word "hope" clearly in its web.

Right now, the winds blow velvety across the canal and the sun is not a giant harsh eye. Sparkling sunshine on miniature canal waves makes me blink myself into a calm state of being here... only here. There is an inherent order in the swirls of tiny fish weaving the icons of their optimism near the canal wall. Even though today the water is filthier than ever, there is a new rhythm to its flow, as if the canal doesn't give a damn what I think. In any case, the water always turns murky after a heavy rain so clarity may be a waste of time.

As I stand on the canal wall looking downward, it feels as if all my innards have been drained into the water and taken elsewhere. Time has a new clock now and it prepares me for the unexpected.

The bank of clouds to the north becomes a duvet that covers me perfectly. I stick out my toes from under the sky quilt until my feet fell just right. Yes, I am getting ready for something and it's not sleep.

Looking east is a reassuring act because its brown and green colours remain constant, even in varying shades of daylight. Tree shadows create a black on green cartoon, as if the sky were doing a shadow puppet story of what's about to happen.

And there it is. A man on the low side of fifty and dressed like Indiana Jones, stops at each bench containing a sleeping, homeless person and prays over each and every dormant form. His praying is occasionally interrupted by a light, light rain followed by more sunbeams. When he leans over a sleeping man under a faded green tarp, the explorer takes extra time for his picture-taking with a high-end camera. Then he leans closer for a second, third and fourth photograph. The clicking wakes the homeless man who says: "Hey, what do you want from me?"

The photographer turns, looks at me and his face wonders what I want too. Then the homeless man looks up and says:" That's me you're taking pictures of, mister."

"How much?" asks the explorer digging into his back pocket of his perfectly wrinkled khakis.

"As long as it's paper and not coins, I'll be happy," the homeless man replies lifting his tarp.

"Paper it is," the photographer says.

The explorer pulls out his Indiana Jones worn wallet and hands the homeless man three perfectly folded but different dollar bills, each one flapping in the sunlight, like flags from three different countries.

"That should do it," the homeless man says tucking the money into his shirt pocket. "So, what are you planning to do with the pictures?"

"I'm hoping to enter them in a magazine contest when I return home."

"Can you win money?" he asks.

"First Prize is a thousand bucks," the photographer says.

"In that case I want a piece of the action if you win, and a copy of the magazine!"

"Of course," says the explorer. "Half-and-half. My wife and I are planning to return next year.

"I'll always be here!" he says. "My face is worth it!"

"Even if I don't win, I'll be back," the photographer says. "I have to. The canal does that to me."

Walking away from the two men, I look over the wall and, half-way down the steps, a spider spins its silken threads with the word "hope" clearly in its web.

BIOGRAPHY: KEN RIVARD

Born and raised in Montreal, Ken Rivard holds a Master's Degree from McGill University and has taught at all levels including Mount Royal University in Calgary. With CANALWATCH, he has published 11 books professionally in various genres including: flash/postcard fiction, poetry, children's literature and the novel. Rivard's books have been finalists for The Writers Guild of Alberta Book Awards including The City of Calgary W.O. Mitchell Book Prize. His writing has appeared in many regional and national publications, in anthologies and on CBC Radio. He has also presented numerous readings and writing workshops across Canada. During 2017-2018, Rivard had the privilege of working as a writing mentor for The Writer's Guild of Alberta Mentorship Writing Program. He has also served as the Writer-in-Residence for both The Calgary Public Library and The Writers Guild of Alberta (Strawberry Creek). His novel, *MOTHERWILD* (2014) was longlisted for Canada's 2015 ReLit Book Award. His website, kenrivard.ca, contains reviews of many of his publications. Ken Rivard lives in Calgary and writing has been in his blood since the first day he learned how to imagine.

"CRITICAL ACCLAIM FOR KEN RIVARD'S WRITING."

Motherwild (novel, 2014)

"Any reader who has gone through life with an addicted family member will relate to the struggles faced by Joey…this is a beautiful book that is sure to tug at the heartstrings of readers everywhere. Lisa MacLean, *Tofts Reviews*

"Unique sense of time and place…which he (Ken Rivard) largely presents without the rose-coloured hue of nostalgia. Eric Volmers, *The Calgary Herald*

"In his 10th book, Ken Rivard shows himself to be a pro at capturing the realities of working class humanity. *Motherwild* is a work of beauty, a coming-of-age story and the eventual healing of a mother-son relationship. Rivard's writing is honest, refreshing, startling, imaginative and gets the reader emotionally involved. *Motherwild* is a really good read!" *W.P Kinsella*

"I enjoyed Motherwild a great deal and I wish you all the success you deserve." *Denys Arcand, Filmmaker*

Missionary Positions (fiction, 2008)

"Developing different protagonists with distinct voices is tough but Rivard pulls it off. A master of imagery… once again Rivard treats these very personal subjects with humanity. *Missionary Positions* reads real, touches readers deeply and hits home on many fronts." Wendy Rajala, *The Calgary Herald*

WHISKEY EYES (fiction, 2004)

"Rivard's flash fiction works...inventive...poetic...all relate to a single narrative arc and thus creating a moving and lasting impression. In an era when more and more people live to an advanced age, many readers are likely to relate to Mark's (the main protagonist) dilemma and find the subtly and humanity with which Rivard treats this very personal, yet universal theme to be a source of comfort and inspiration. "K. Gordon Neufeld, *The Calgary Herald*

"An intense book that deals with the substantial emotional involvement stemming from the responsibility of caring for aging parents." Jennifer Partridge, *The Calgary Herald*

"Demonstrates the problem when those aged parents become the children...a difficult problem handled brilliantly. Kirk Layton, *Chapters/Indigo Website*

BOTTLE TALK (fiction, 2002)

"An excellent display of Rivard's talent as a writer. It is dynamic and sincere and although it is connected by a common thread of alcoholism, the ugly truths that Rivard forces us to view with eyes wide open, are not just those of alcoholism but the basic truths of humanity and life. Heather Doody, *Candian Book Review Annual*

"Intensely written with compelling, graphic honesty, Rivard is an astute observer. Reading this book is like probing an open wound that has not healed. It is a brilliant collection of truth and glimpses into one's very soul." Anne Burke, *Praire Journal of Canadian Literature*

MOM, THE SCHOOL FLOODED (children's literature, 1995)

"The book's success is based on its perfect marriage of text and illustration. Ken Rivard's closing dialogue involves the reader in the creative process providing firsthand experience of creative storytelling." Christine Linge, *CM Magazine*

"Young readers will enjoy watching someone else test the boundaries of credibility." Diane Fitzgerald, *CM Magazine*

"Readers are left with a brilliant illustration to let their minds solve the rest of the story and is an excellent story to add to your collection." John Dryden, *CM Magazine*

"A remarkable story about a school gone wet." Katherine Garber, *SMS Book Reviews*

SKIN TESTS (fiction, 2000). Finalist for The Writers Guild of Alberta Short Fiction Award and The City of Calgary W.O. Mitchell Book Prize. Write your own online review...if you wish.

IF SHE COULD TAKE ALL THESE MEN (fiction, 1995). Finalist for The Writers' Guild of Alberta Short Fiction Award.

"Amazing collection…captures a poignant vignette from the life of an extraordinary ordinary person. Such thought-provoking portraits bring alive a diverse representation of humanity and render the reader party to intense moments in private lives…does an absorbing and competent job of conjuring entire lives in these micro-bites of narrative. Virginia Gillham, *Canadian Book Review Annual*

“The pleasure is opening one door after another onto lives quickly drawn, sketches of characters caught in odd moments neither random nor monumental. It is this interpretation of lives, this ever-latent potential for changing places, that I find the most engaging quality of this collection, though adroit descriptions are another. The reader will be drawn in by curiosity as to what or who might appear next…exemplary…funny…mysterious…quite wonderful. Roo Borson, *Books in Canada*

“Exciting and well-crafted…Rivard’s short short stories are carefully written narratives that provide glimpses into the lives of some very unusual people…poignant…heartbreaking and honest…the best capture the telling moments of life with humour and compassion…engaging.” Debbie Howlett, *Quill & Quire*

FRANKIE’S DESIRES (poetry, 1987).

“Rivard feels closer to the down and out than to the high and mighty. Frankie, whose frank desires, devilish sense of humour and ironic awareness of his own devilishness, makes the book lively. Rivard is a fine reporter of the foibles of this protagonist. The wit is rich and typical of the tone of this artfully sophisticated but innocent even simple looking work. Like Frost before him, Rivard is touching the heart with Frankie’s apparent naivete, only pretending to be Everyman. This lovely, lively, loving work will be the most important repositioning of a Canadian poet to appear this year…establishes him (Rivard) as a powerful writer and this collection is recommended for libraries with Commonwealth, Canadian and contemporary shelves. Rivard, the Calgary poet of the unforgettable Frankie will be heard from again and again.” Robert Solomon *SMALL PRESS*

“Frankie ain’t beautiful but he’s audaciously real.” Mark Lowey, *THE CALGARY HERALD*

"Ken Rivard's poems are sad/funny reflections of ourselves as we dream-desire our way through the maze that is defined as life. His verse lines echo in the ears of all who would listen to him." Michael O'Nowlan, *Canadian Book Review Annual*

"FRANKIE"S DESIRES becomes ours- to live- to open up to- to understand." Gerald Hill, *The Edmonton Journal*

KISS ME DOWN TO SIZE (poetry, 1983)

"Sense of commitment...written from the engaged stance of an observing human being in this world. Rivard keeps a trained eye (and ear) on the emotional energy that lies in wait beneath the lines. It is not written by a pompous poet in capital letters. Its voice is gentle, insistent in its quiet way and everywhere fraught with a concurrent sense of humility and necessity." Judith Fitzgerald, *Canadian Literature*

"Rivard has a good sense of when to spin out and where it should go. And he nicely flips a surreal attachment to many of his statements." Michael Cullen, *Out of the Blue*

"Presents with bracing force a regional voice that is astringent-almost impossible to ignore." Allan Hustak, *Alberta Report*

"Writes in simple, colloquial diction...uses spare language, an unadorned style." Anne Burke, *Writers Quarterly*

"Rivard's essential humanism is obvious...(Rivard) is able to write emphatically about elderly and young alike...diction and imagery are strong and pleasing." Martin Singleton, *Canadian Book Review Annual*

"The most impressive aspect of Rivard's work is its tendency towards a surrealistic, dream-like quality." Bob Attridge, *Newest Annual*